THE
ENFORCER

Novelization by
Wesley Morgan

From a screenplay by
Gail Hickman and
S. W. Shurr, Sterling Silliphant,
Dean Riesner. Based on the Character
created by Harry Julian Fink
and Rita M. Fink

A STAR BOOK

published by
the Paperback Division of
W. H. ALLEN & Co. Ltd.

A Star Book
Published in 1978
by the Paperback Division of
W. H. Allen & Co. Ltd
A Howard and Wyndham Company
44 Hill Street, London W1X 8LB
Reprinted 1980

Originally published in the United States
by Warner Books, Inc., 1976

Printed in Great Britain by
Richard Clay (The Chaucer Press) Ltd
Bungay, Suffolk

ISBN 0 352 30239 9

For Clint.
Thanks, amigo.

One

It was the middle of March and it was hot. The temperature had been steadily climbing for hours, and by noon it was into the high nineties. If that was not bad enough, today there was no cooling wind blowing in from the ocean, only an occasional flutter of hot air that did nothing to help the situation. Scorched stale air washed over everything. Television meteorologists reported the heat wave would continue unabated until the weekend.

Standing by the side of the road, Miki felt the heat radiating from the tar blacktop of the highway, blasting her slim body like a furnace. Even wearing Levi's cut off at the thighs and a halter top with no bra underneath, she was uncomfortable to the point of misery. She could feel the perspiration beading in her shoulder blades, dribbling down her long spine to form an itching wet spot in the small of her back. The heat made her light-headed, almost high. It was the way she felt after one or two hits off that strong Cambodian grass Bobby had. Only that was a good feeling, and this was a bummer. And the heat was getting worse.

Miki wiped a hand across her forehead in a futile attempt at relief. She stared at the blazing sun above. God, how hot was it, anyway? Ninety-five? At least that. Maybe a hundred. The weather report had predicted it might reach that high. It was like standing at the gates of hell.

To passersby Miki Waleska looked like a pretty young college co-ed, the kind college boys have fantasies about. Her hair was blond, her eyes were wide and blue, and she had the attractive slimness that promised never to grow fat and sloppy with age. Her breasts were a little on the small side, but well-formed. Her legs were long, tanned, with a nice, tapered shape. Her pert, upturned nose was dotted with freckles as a final touch. She might have been someone's grownup kid sister.

She was, in fact, a hooker.

At twenty-three Miki had been hooking for nearly three years now. It wasn't something that she could honestly say she enjoyed doing, but then again, it wasn't something she despised, either. It was a job, and you had to view a job from a practical point of view. You spent a lot of time on your back and some time on your feet. If you were good—and Miki knew she was good—the hours were short and the pay was good. It was a hell of a lot better than busting your butt as a secretary or waitress or some other stupid forty-hour-a-week gig. It was easy, and she had a natural talent for it. Men had always been attracted to her, since she'd outgrown her training bra at fourteen. Probably it was that young, innocent look that appealed to them so much.

Not that there weren't drawbacks. Sometimes the Johns hassled you or tried to get rough. Some of them had pretty funny ideas about what they could get for their money. But then there was Bobby, and he usually took care of any problems like that. And there were the busts. In the past year Miki had been busted twice. Bobby had taken care of that, too, posting her bail, hiring a lawyer, paying her fines. Bobby always took care of his girls, watched over them, protected them. He was a fantastic person. As long as there was Bobby, life would be cool.

A bright red Cadillac convertible appeared at the turn down the road. Automatically Miki stuck out her thumb and tightened her thighs. The Cadillac slowed as it approached, nosing over to the side of the road.

An older man with a pencil mustache and thinning hair stuck his head out of the window. Miki felt his eyes flicking across her bare midriff and tight crotch. A twerp. The kind who had a lot of bizarre ideas in the sack but didn't want to pay for it.

"Hey, you sure look like you could use a lift," he said through a nervous grin. "Where exactly you headed, baby?"

Miki eyed him coldly, taking her time, letting him sweat. In a voice that could have taken the paint off his car, she snarled, "Nowhere with you, you fat asshole. Now fuck off!"

The driver turned an unattractive red, his grin fading away. "Bitch!" he growled, then slid back behind the wheel. The Cadillac squealed off down the road, leaving the stink of burned rubber and a cloud of dust behind it. The driver stuck his hand out of the window, middle finger held high for her to see.

"Eat it, needle prick!" Miki screamed after him. The Cadillac disappeared. Miki snorted and continued walking. Turkey-necked jerk!

A hundred yards farther on, Miki stopped in front of a roadside diner. A sign on the front announced that this was *George and Irma's Truckstop Food*. It was an old, weatherworn, once off-white building with dirty windows and peeling paint. Country music from the jukebox filtered out through the screen door. Johnny Cash singing about trucks and truckers. Life and death on the endless road. Through the window Miki could see two men inside at the counter, talking to the waitress.

Miki smiled to herself, as if laughing at some private, inner joke. She turned her attention to the single vehicle parked in the dirt lot in front of the diner. It was a dark brown utility truck with the elliptical emblem of the Western Gas Company painted on the side. It was one of those high, square-built jobs, the kind that are used for delivering equipment. She eyed it curiously for a moment, then sank down on a large rock by the shoulder of the road to wait. The rock was hot, and Miki found herself shifting around to keep her legs from

7

being burned. She closed her eyes and tried to lick some life into her dry lips, hating the unbearable heat.

She did not have to wait for very long. In a few minutes the screen door of the diner slapped open, and the two men she had seen through the window stepped out into the parking lot. Both were dressed in gas company uniforms. The younger of the two, with curly blond hair and a bright, cheerful smile, leaned back through the open doorway for a moment. In a good-natured voice he called, "See you next Thursday, if I can hold myself back that long, you gorgeous thing!" As he let the door slam the faint sound of the waitress's laughter drifted after him, mixing with the music from the jukebox. The young man quick-stepped to catch up to his older partner, who was grinning.

"How do you do it, Johnny?" the older man asked.

The younger man, Johnny, broadened his grin and slapped his friend on the back. "Don't you know by now? It's my charm, man. It's a gift. The women just eat it up like it was candy."

The older man looked at him sourly. "If you have charm, then I'm a duck."

"I hate to say this, Andy, old buddy, but I have noticed a definite resemblance."

"I'm flattered you took time to look."

"It's mostly in your walk."

Approaching the utility truck, Johnny saw Miki stand up, stick her thumb out, and start walking backwards toward them. He gazed appreciatively at her long legs and tight, round behind. Nice, he thought, very, very nice.

As Miki went past them Johnny flashed her his most winning smile. "You sure picked one hell of a hot day to go hitchhiking," he told her.

Miki stopped, smiling back at him. "Don't I know it! I just know I'm going to die from this damned heat. It must be at least ninety-five today."

"Ninety-eight. I just heard it on the radio." It was a lie, but it was a good way of making conversation. Johnny considered himself an expert in the art of making conversation with pretty girls.

8

Miki brushed the hair out of her face with a practiced flip of her hand. "It's a bad day for me," she said in a tone of admission. "I cracked the block of my VW bug down on Stinson Beach. I got it towed to a service station back up the road, and now I'm hitching my way home."

Johnny looked at Andy, who was eyeing him with impatience, in a hurry to get going. Sometimes the old man just didn't have any heart at all, no idea how to take it easy and enjoy himself. All he ever thought about was his job. As far as Johnny was concerned, there were other things in life.

Johnny turned back to Miki. "Where you headed, anyway?"

"Mill Valley Road. I've got a little place in the canyon there." Her forehead wrinkled quizzically. "Hey, you guys wouldn't be going up that way, would you? I haven't had very much luck today getting a ride. I'd sure appreciate it if you could give me a lift."

Johnny glanced back at his partner. "Hey, we're going up past Mill Valley Road, aren't we?"

Andy cocked one eyebrow in disbelief. "Mill Valley Road? You're really something else, you know that? That's way the hell out of our way. Besides, we're not supposed to have passengers in the truck."

Johnny grinned sheepishly, shrugging. "Aw, come on. What the hell does it matter? It's not that far."

"Look, we've got all that equipment to deliver in Sausalito still." Andy pulled back his sleeve and looked pointedly at his watch. "It's nearly two now. We don't make that delivery, the boss is going to be one mad bastard."

"We've got the time," insisted Johnny. "It's only a couple of miles out of our way. How much time can it take? Nobody is going to know. We can just say that Tiburon job took us a little longer than we expected. You know they aren't going to call up and check us on it."

"I've got a couple of bottles of ice-cold beer up at the cabin, if you'd be interested," put in Miki hopefully. "I sure would appreciate a ride in this heat."

9

"Come on," said Johnny, nudging Andy. "It's hot."

Andy considered for a moment, and Johnny knew he had him. Finally the older man nodded. "Yeah, okay, I guess so," he sighed. "But just a quick one, and then we have to go." He glanced at Miki, who favored him with a beaming smile. Nodding at the truck he said, "Okay, pile in. Let's get going. We haven't got all day, you know."

The three of them climbed into the truck, Miki between the two men. Andy started the engine and pulled out onto the highway.

"I'm Johnny and this is Andy," said Johnny, lighting up a cigarette. He offered one to Miki. She shook her head.

"I don't smoke."

"What's your name?"

Miki paused briefly before answering, wondering if she should give them a false name. She decided it didn't really matter in the long run, since neither of them would ever tell anyone. "Miki," she said.

Johnny laughed. "Mickey? As in Mickey Mouse?"

Miki grimaced, shaking her head. "You know how many times people have pulled that same old joke on me? That was even my nickname in high school. I've only heard it maybe a million times."

"And here I thought I was being clever."

"It's okay. I don't really mind. I've gotten used to it by now, I've heard it so many times. Anyway, that's not the way it's spelled. It's M-I-K-I."

"That's kind of unusual. I think I like it." Johnny took a long drag on his cigarette. "Hey, I'm willing to bet you were a cheerleader when you were in school, right?"

"I was," admitted Miki. "How did you guess?"

Johnny ran his eyes over her. "Oh, you just look like the cheerleader type. Where did you go to high school?"

"Palo Alto."

"Oh, yeah?" Johnny was pleased. "I was born and raised in Redwood City. We were practically neighbors. I lettered in basketball and track."

Miki nodded, feigning enthusiasm. He looked like an ex-jock, all right. "That's really interesting." It wasn't. She had heard the same line many times before. But she knew Johnny was eating it up. Stringing guys along was part of the trade; Miki had learned that a long time ago. This was going to be so easy. She leaned back, smiling to herself. Everything was going just as Bobby had said it would, just as he had planned.

At twenty-eight Bobby Maxwell was an arresting sight. His shoulder-length blond hair was full and blond and beautiful, more like a girl's than a man's. He was tall, powerfully built, deeply tanned, and handsome by almost anyone's standards. When he moved, it was as a cat moves, with the contained physical prowess and grace of a trained athlete. But the most impressive things about Bobby were his eyes. Intense, almost wild, not quite concealing an inner savagery that was downright frightening, they were the eyes of a hunter. Bobby's generally calm, casual exterior belied his ability for violence. Bobby Maxwell was a killer.

Sitting under a tree in front of the small cabin, leaning back easily against the trunk, Bobby dreamed about being rich. He had always known that someday he would be rich. It was a matter of timing, of being in the right place at the right time when the right opportunity came along. When that time came, you had to be ruthless enough to take advantage of it, regardless of what was involved. It was a hard, brutal world, Bobby knew, and you had to be tougher than the others if you wanted to make it. That was something he firmly believed. It was the only rule, the secret of success. Never let anything or anyone stand in your way. If you saw something you wanted, you took it. If some fool tried to get between you and what you wanted, you killed him. It was that simple. Fuck the others and take care of number one. That was the only way to survive. Bobby Maxwell was a survivor.

His head jerked up sharply at the sound of an approaching engine, like an animal taking a scent. He listened a moment, head cocked toward the sound, recognizing the truck engine. That meant Miki had done her job.

Bobby leaped smoothly to his feet, scooping up the shotgun that had been lying on the ground beside him. He moved off into the shadows at the side of the cabin in an easy trot. He pulled back out of sight to wait. Down the road he saw the utility truck slowly wind its way up to the cabin. In a few minutes it pulled to a halt in the dirt driveway.

Johnny clambered out of the cab, gallantly offering his hand to help Miki down. He looked at the old wooden house and garage, built right on the edge of a cliff at a dead-end turnaround. A nice little out-of-the-way spot. He was going to make a point to remember where it was.

"This is nice," he said. "You have a great view of the whole valley from up here." He grinned. "Must be great at night," he added.

"It needs a little work," said Miki ."Actually, I inherited it from my grandmother. I'm trying to get it fixed up, but there's so much to do. Everything costs too much nowadays. There's no way I can afford to pay anyone to do the work, so I have to do it all myself. I work at it in my spare time, but that's really slow going."

"Yeah, I know what you mean. Hey, I'm a handy man with a paintbrush and a hammer. I've got a pickup truck to haul things with. If you ever need anybody to help you out, I want you to know that I'm available."

"I'm just liable to take you up on that, you know."

"The offer stands."

Miki started toward the house. "Come on. I owe you two a couple of beers."

Johnny followed her. Andy climbed out of the driver's side, mopping at his forehead with an old sweat-stained red neckerchief.

"I'll be right with you," said Andy tiredly. "I've got to take that radiator cap off before the whole damned engine burns up. You got any water here, miss?"

Miki stopped by the front door. She pointed to a

coiled green hose at the side of the garage. "There's a hose over there. You can help yourself. You need a pair of pliers to turn on the water, though. There isn't any knob. It's one of those things I've been meaning to fix but haven't got around to yet."

"I've got pliers."

Miki and Johnny went into the house. Andy walked slowly around to the front of the truck and looked at it with disgust. He lifted the heavy hood, propping it up with a hinged metal rod. The radiator was steaming. Carefully he wrapped the red neckerchief around the radiator cap, trying to loosen it without burning his hand. As he turned the cap there was a sudden blast of steam from the release valve. Andy cursed loudly, rubbing his scalded fingers.

Standing as he was, with his back to the house, he did not see Bobby Maxwell hidden in the shadows, watching him. For nearly a minute Bobby did not move, quietly contemplating the man in front of him. The man he was going to kill. Not that Bobby had the slightest sadness or twinge of conscience about the prospect of killing. He did not. In fact, quite the reverse, he enjoyed the idea. Killing gave Bobby a charge, gave him a high more fantastic than any drug he had ever taken. It excited him the way some men are excited by sex. He could vividly remember the first time he had ever killed a man, a Vietcong sniper hidden in the muck of a rice paddy near Da Nang. Bobby had slipped up behind the man quietly, grabbing his mouth with one hand, driving the knife into the abdomen with the other, exactly as he had been taught in the Special Forces training school. It had been so easy. The sniper stared up at him, eyes uncomprehending and frightened, not willing to believe his own impending death, but knowing. Then blood gurgled out of his mouth and he died. One moment he had been a living, breathing human being; the next he was nothing but a lifeless lump of useless flesh. Dead meat, nothing more. At that moment Bobby's head had begun to spin and his ears had begun to buzz. He was transported, feeling a surge of power course through his body like electricity, filling him with a new strength, giving him life. Since that time Bobby had killed others. Some in Vietnam, Some in the United States. But always he felt the same extraordinary feeling when he did, and always, always he enjoyed it.

He remembered that feeling now as he noiselessly slid up behind the man at the truck, easing the commando knife out of its oiled scabbard. With the methodical precision of a trained killer, Bobby snapped his hand over Andy's mouth, jamming the knife into Andy's gut to the hilt, up under the lower ribs, piercing the heart. The Gas Company man jerked spasmodically as his insides fell apart. Bobby held him tightly as he shuddered and finally went limp, becoming dead weight. It was all over very quickly, in the space of a few seconds, Bobby closed his eyes, his whole body tingling with excitement, his pulse pounding furiously against his temples. He was a man falling through space from ten miles up. He was a bolt of lightning streaking through the clouds. He was god.

Forcing himself back to reality, Bobby carefully eased the body to the ground, taking care not to get any blood on his clothes. He wiped the blood off the knife blade onto the dead man's shirt, then returned the knife to its scabbard. Andy lay on his back in a thickening pool of dark blood, his mouth pulled open in an endless silent scream that no one would ever hear. In death, like all men, he had become ugly.

Bobby crossed back to the shadows of the house where he had hidden. He picked up the shotgun he had left there. Inside he could hear the voices of Miki and Johnny, laughing at some joke. He moved to the nearest window. In the kitchen he saw the two of them standing by the sink, very close together, eyes locked on each other. Johnny leaned forward to kiss Miki lightly on the lips. She pushed him away, not angrily, but playfully. She said something in a low voice that Bobby could not quite make out, nodding toward the door, and then the two of them were laughing again.

Bobby pulled away from the window, going back along the side of the house through the shadows. He

14

walked to the utility truck, stepping around the body, not even bothering to glance at it. Leaning through the open cab window he banged the heel of his hand hard on the horn, giving three quick blasts that echoed through the canyon. Then he leaned comfortably against the truck, raising the shotgun. He thumbed back both hammers gently, enjoying the soft metallic click they made.

In a few moments Johnny appeared in the cabin doorway. He was still laughing, pleased with the way another dull working day had developed into something else entirely. "Hey, Andy, what the hell is taking you so long? Don't you want some—"

He froze as he saw Andy's stiffening body lying on the ground. Johnny's jaw dropped open. He tried to look away, but couldn't. "Jesus, oh God," he whispered, shaking his head in disbelief. He was unable to really comprehend what he was seeing. The beer in his stomach turned to bile, and he felt it rise toward his throat. He was going to be sick. He swallowed back his vomit and tore his eyes away from Andy.

He saw Bobby Maxwell leaning against the truck, smiling, shotgun leveled at him. The twin muzzles looked like two gaping tunnels. He knew then that he was going to die.

"Don't kill me," moaned Johnny in terror, putting up his hands. "God, please don't kill me. I don't even know you. Whatever you want, take it. I don't care, just don't kill me." He waited for an answer, but Bobby said nothing, just kept smiling. "You want my wallet? I'll give you my wallet. I only have forty dollars, but you can have it, okay? It's everything I've got." Johnny fumbled his wallet out of his back pocket with trembling fingers. He pulled out the bills, dropping the wallet, holding the green paper out for Bobby to see. "Here, look, it's all there is, I swear. It's yours." He started toward Bobby, feet shuffling almost comically, like a character out of an old minstrel show. His voice became a whimper. "Go ahead, please. Go ahead and take it—"

He never finished. The shotgun blast took him full

15

in the face and chest, nearly taking off his head, slamming him back into the dirt. He was dead before he hit the ground.

Miki came out of the cabin. She looked down dispassionately at the two grisly bodies on the ground in front of her. Already flies were beginning to gather, attracted by the coppery smell of blood that hung heavy in the air.

Bobby lowered the shotgun and walked toward Miki.

"How did I do?" she asked in a voice that pleaded for approval.

"You did good. Very good. Now let's get these bodies out of here. We can bury them in that ravine down the canyon. Then we call the others and tell them everything went okay."

Miki nodded absently. "Yes, Bobby."

Bobby looked down at her with his intense eyes. He reached out and stroked her cheek softly with the back of his hand. Miki smiled.

"I feel good," Bobby said.

Two

From the sky San Francisco is a vast and impressive sight. The Golden Gate Bridge dominates the bay, gleaming bright orange in the sun. Coit Tower on Telegraph Hill juts proudly at the sky. Nearby, the elongated, pyramid-shaped TransAmerica Building, amid the sprawl of the downtown skyscrapers, looks like a NASA rocket poised for takeoff. The streets of famous Chinatown and North Beach are always jammed with tourists moving like thousands of army ants. Freighters, sailboats, and tourist cruisers cover the glittering bay. Even the grim gray walls of Alcatraz seem harmless, resembling some fairy tale castle on a mythical island. It is a city of astonishing beauty and splendor which, but for the steel buildings and concrete streets, might be an ancient, golden port out of Marco Polo's imagination.

All of this, however, was lost on Harry Callahan as he wheeled the unmarked police car on to Bay Street and headed west. As an inspector with the homicide division of the San Francisco Police Department, Harry saw his surroundings as simply a city filled with killers, thieves, muggers, rapists, pimps, pushers, hookers, con men, and the like. Where the wandering tourist saw grace and beauty, Harry saw a breeding ground of crime. After nearly twenty years with the force, Harry was well acquainted with the darker side of San Francisco. He knew the dark alleys and the cathouses, the massage parlors and the slum apartment buildings, the dollar-a-night hotels and the sleazy bars. Statistics showed that major crime offenses in the city had nearly doubled in the last five years. Murders were up over ten percent from the same period last year. Rapes were up twenty-six percent. Robbery up thirty-eight percent. Aggravated assault up twenty-six percent. Burglary up forty-two percent. Larceny up twenty-nine percent. Auto thef up thirty-one percent. It went on and on, up and up. A man could go crazy just keeping up with the numbers. It was depressing. As a member of one of the finest police forces in the world, Harry faced the grim fact that things were getting worse, not better. Nor was San Francisco any different than any other major urban area in the United States. The situation was the same everywhere. Given the present continuing trends, in twenty years the cities would be unlivable.

"Say, Harry."

Harry looked over at his partner, fat Frank Di-Georgio, who was listening to a tiny transistor radio. "What?"

"How would you like to come over for dinner tomorrow night?" DiGeorgio asked in a casual voice. "Irene says she'll make lasagna the way you like it."

Harry eyed his partner with sidelong suspicion. "Who is it this time?"

"Who is what?" asked DiGeorgio innocently.

"The chick you've got lined up for me to meet."

"Chick?"

"Come on, Frank. Don't kid a kidder."

DiGeorgio looked injured. "Hey, Harry, would I do that? Set you up? We're pals, right?"

"Yeah, rights. Pals," said Harry. "Who's the chick?"

"Harry, I wouldn't con you."

"You wouldn't, but Irene would. She's always trying to fix me up with somebody or other. We both know she thinks I should get married again. Last month it was that divorcée with two kids. That was cute. Before that it was Vivian What's-her-name, the schoolteacher who lives with her mother. You know what I'm talking about. It isn't just a coincidence that every time I come

18

over for dinner there's some chick there for me to meet. So who is she, Frank?"

DiGeorgio sighed with resignation. He had known it wouldn't work. He had told Irene. Why did he let her talk him into these things? "She's some friend of Irene's," he said finally. "I think she's a librarian. Irene thinks that the two of you would be perfect for each other."

"Perfect. Great."

DiGeorgio nodded his head slightly to one side. "She's not bad-looking, Harry. Nice legs."

Harry was unconvinced. "A librarian," he muttered. "Outstanding."

The police radio crackled with static. "Rear-end collision on Cervantes Boulevard," buzzed the voice ot the communications officer. Harry recognized it as belonging to Sergeant Tom Miller, an old friend from the Police Academy. "Traffic officers on the scene. Traffic is beginning to back up—advise all cars to take alternate routes."

"Better hang a left here, Harry," DiGeorgio suggested.

Harry nodded and made a hard turn. A taxicab-yellow Mustang squealed out of a service station driveway, cutting right in front of them. Harry hit the brakes to avoid a collision. He slammed the palm of his hand angrily on the horn, then yelled out of the window, "Watch where the hell you're going, bullet-head!"

The driver of the Mustang ignored the epithet, roaring off down the street in a cloud of exhaust, oblivious to everything but himself and his car.

"Jesus," muttered Harry disgustedly, "look at all that pollution. Somebody ought to take a baseball bat and ram it up his—"

He broke off as something caught his eye up ahead. A white-jacketed waiter with a look of extreme panic on his face rushed out of the front door of the Place Pigalle restaurant, eyes darting anxiously up and down the street. A crowd was beginning to gather behind him around the restaurant door, craning their necks to see inside.

"Something's up," Harry said. pulling over to the curb. He glanced out at the waiter. "I'm a cop," Harry told him. "What's the problem here?"

The waiter wrung his hands worriedly. "Thank God!" He bobbed his head in the direction of the restaurant. "One of our customers just had a heart attack. Just fell over on the table. He's in a bad way. We sent for an ambulance ten minutes ago, but it's still not here. None of us know what to do for the poor man. Can you help?"

"I'll see what I can do." Harry looked at his partner. "I'll handle it." He opened the door and climbed out.

The waiter led the way through the crowd at the door. Inside, the restaurant was dark and cool, a welcome relief from the blistering heat outside. Harry shoved his way through the knot of diners and waiters clustered in a semicircle near the back of the room.

"Police. Move back."

The crowd parted for him. The unconscious heart-attack victim lay on the floor, the unpaid bill clutched tightly in one fist, his face red, his mouth wide open, and gasping for breath like a beached fish. In the agony of his attack he had overturned his table and chair, spilling plates, silverware, and glasses all over the floor.

Harry nodded at the maitre d', a fattish man with a carefully trimmed mustache. He had the sour expression of a man who wished this had happened someplace else. A waiter knelt by the unconscious man, loosening his tie and collar.

"Where is the ambulance?" demanded the maitre d' of Harry, as if he was one of the hired help.

"You won't need it," Harry replied. He started kicking the man on the floor in the ribs. "Come on, time to go. Get up, get up."

The waiter looked up, horrified. "What are you doing? My God, he's had a heart attack. You'll kill him!"

Harry ignored the waiter's protests and continued kicking. "Come on, Eddie. Get your ass up."

The man on the floor groaned audibly, his eyes fluttering open. He wheezed painfully.

Harry kicked harder. "I said let's go. On your feet and cut the crap."

The waiter and the others looked on in horrified silence. Still the man on the floor did not move. Harry gave him a final sharp kick, then reached down and gathered a fistful of necktie. The man made a strangling sound. Harry yanked him violently to his feet.

"Cancel the ambulance," advised Harry as he dragged the choking customer out the door.

Outside Harry glared at the crowd. "All right, that's it, fun's over. Nobody died, better luck next time."

The crowd lingered for a second, still wondering what was going on, then began to disperse. Harry let go of the customer's necktie. The man gasped for air.

"Jesus, Harry," wheezed the man, running his hand around his chafed throat, "you nearly choked me to death!"

Harry scowled. "You got your free dinner, Eddie. So what are you squawking about?"

The con man grinned, then shrugged. "I always kind of enjoy the ambulance ride."

"No free rides today," Harry growled. "Just get your ass out of here before I kick it up around your ears. Count yourself lucky that I don't take you in for vagrancy. And I better not catch you hanging around here again, or I'm going to use your head for a football. Savvy?"

Eddie nodded. "Yeah, Harry, sure. You know how it is, I'm just a little down on my luck right now." He shifted his feet uncomfortably and ran his fingers over his chin. "You . . . uh . . . reckon you could loan me a couple of bucks? Just for a few days. I'll pay you back the next time I see you—honest."

Harry glared at Eddie. Disgustedly he pulled his wallet out and withdrew a five-dollar bill.

"Hey, thanks, Harry," said Eddie with heartfelt gratitude. "I won't forget this, believe me. I really appreciate you helping me out this way. And I'll pay you back just as soon as I can." He snatched up the bill, folded it, and stuffed it into his coat pocket.

"Yeah, yeah," snarled Harry. He spun the con man around then gave him a boot in the backside with the side of his foot, sending him down the street at a gallop.

As Harry climbed back into the unmarked police car, he saw DiGeorgio was grinning from ear to ear.

"You're tough, Harry," DiGeorgio chuckled. "Really tough."

"Kiss my ass," said Harry. He shifted into gear and pulled out into traffic.

"About that dinner—"

"Forget it. I'm not coming. I don't need a girl friend. I know lots of women."

"Who?"

"None of your goddamn business."

"Ah, come on, Harry," DiGeorgio pleaded. "It's just a dinner. Nobody says you've got to marry the girl. Besides, if you don't come, Irene won't talk to me for a week."

"I said no."

"What are you going to do? Cry the blues about Louise all your life? When are you going to get her out of your system?"

Harry's jaw tightened: "Maybe never. But it's my business."

DiGeorgio was silent for a few moments. At last he said, "Look, we've been friends for a long time, right?"

Harry grimaced. "If you're going to give me the speech about how I owe you one, don't bother. We're friends, but I'm still not going. So let's just drop it."

"Okay," agreed DiGeorgio, "I won't push it. But if you change your mind—"

"Will you shut the hell up?"

"All right, already." DiGeorgio turned his attention to the passing traffic. "Speaking of food, how about we stop somewhere and get a bite to eat? I'm hungry."

Harry glanced at his partner's portly frame. "Hungry? You've got enough meat on you to feed an army. When are you going to lose some weight, fatso?"

22

"It's Irene's cooking. She loves to cook and I love to eat. I can't help myself. I keep putting on the pounds. Starting next week, I think I'll start going down to the police gym to work out. You want to come along?"

"No, thanks."

"How do you manage to stay so skinny, anyway? You never put on any weight—and you eat like a horse."

Harry shrugged. "I thought you knew. I take Geritol."

At the next corner Harry pulled into a Doggie Diner. He ordered two quarter-pound cheeseburgers with everything and a big Coke, while DiGeorgio asked for a chili dog and an order of fries.

Back in the car Harry was just finishing the first cheeseburger when DiGeorgio turned up a call on the radio.

"All units," crackled the radio. "All units. We have a ten-thirteen in progress at the corner of Geary and California. All units. All units. A ten-thirteen in progress at the corner of Geary and California This is a code two red."

"That's us, fatso," Harry said, mouth full of food. He wolfed down the rest of the cheeseburger in one big bite, then twisted the key in the ignition. The engine roared to life.

"Nuts," said DiGeorgio, glancing at his watch. "It's nearly five. Looks like I'm going to be late again. Irene's going to kill me. She's doing a nine church novena, and I told her I'd be home early."

"Life is tough," Harry shot back, screeching out of the driveway.

Five minutes later the police car eased to a halt behind a cluster of black-and-whites at the corner of Geary and California. Just beyond this two white-uniformed attendants were easing a young rookie on a stretcher into the back of an ambulance.

Harry and DiGeorgio piled out, heading for a police sergeant crouched behind one of the cars.

23

"I'm Callahan," said Harry, flashing his star to the sergeant. "What's the trouble?"

The sergeant pointed at a liquor store about halfway down the block. "Some bastards held up that liquor store. One of our guys, Officer Ballou, stumbled onto the thing. They shot him up pretty bad and grabbed four hostages. They say they're going to start shooting the hostages one by one if we don't give them a car and let them go."

The ambulance pulled away down the street, red light flashing, siren beginning to whine. Harry watched it go, then turned back to the sergeant.

"What are you waiting for?"

"Lieutenant Bressler, he says to stall them until he gets here. They've got a Tac Squad on the way."

Harry made a face. "Shit . . ."

There was a commotion at the front of the liquor store. A young man with long hair, a dark-complexioned Chicano, appeared in the doorway, holding a frightened old black woman in front of him. With his other hand he had a sawed-off shotgun jammed up against the side of her head.

"Oh, sweet Jesus," moaned the black woman in terror, "please don't let them kill me!"

The Chicano dragged the old woman out into the middle of the street. "Listen, all you pigs!" he shouted. "You better get that goddamn car over here right now, or we're gonna start killing people!"

Harry grabbed the sergeant's bullhorn and stood up. "You're not getting anything or going anywhere until I come in and talk to you!"

The Chicano hesitated, then nodded. "Okay—we'll talk. But just to you. Nobody else. And put your piece on the hood of that car where I can see it!"

Harry pulled a big Smith and Wesson forty-four out of his bulky shoulder holster and placed it on the hood of the black-and-white. He walked around the front end of the car and halted.

"Okay, pig," shouted the Chicano, "come on in!" He backed into the liquor store, dragging the old woman with him. The door slammed behind him.

Harry started toward the store.

"Hey," called DiGeorgio, "what about me? I'm your partner, remember?"

"You stay here," Harry replied. "If I have to run for it, I don't want any fat guineas in my way."

"You've got a lot of class, Harry. What do you suppose makes a man go crazy enough to join the cops, anyway?"

"If you find out, let me know."

DiGeorgio watched Harry move on down the street. "Watch yourself. I hate going to funerals."

Harry paused in front of the liquor store. It was a good-sized building, flanked on one side by an insurance office and by a laundromat on the other. Reflections in the plate-glass window made it impossible to see inside.

The door opened and Harry went in. As he came through the door a shotgun jabbed into his face. Harry stopped in mid-step. He saw the shotgun was being held by a young Chinese hood wearing a leather jacket.

"Hold it right there, you pig motherfucker," snarled the hood.

Harry froze. Ahead of him he could see the Chicano, also aiming a shotgun at him. Against the wall were the four hostages: the old black woman, a clerk, an older man who looked like he was probably the owner, and a young woman in blue jeans. They were being guarded by two more punks. One was a white kid, not more than twenty, with a face pockmarked by acne. The other was another Chicano, whose face was flat and pushed in from being broken several times.

"On the floor, pig," ordered the leader.

Harry looked at the dirty floor dubiously. "You want me to get down there?"

"For God's sake, mister," wailed the terrified black woman, "you better do like they say, or they'll kill you!"

"This is my good suit," explained Harry. "I just got it out of the cleaners."

"The leader moved forward. "I said get your ass on the deck, you dirty son of a bitch! Now!"

25

The Chinese hood jabbed Harry in the stomach with the shotgun. "Move it, man—do like he says."

With a sigh Harry got down on the floor. The leader came forward and put the shotgun against Harry's face, right under his nose.

"Spread-eagle your arms and legs!"

Harry spread out. The Chinese hood put down his own shotgun, out of Harry's reach, and frisked the front of Harry's suit, starting with his chest, working his way down his legs to his feet.

When he had finished, the leader ordered Harry to roll over. Harry did. The Chinese hood frisked his back quickly.

"He's clean," the hood announced finally. He backed away, picking up his shotgun.

"Okay, bastard," growled the leader, "you listen to me good. First, we want all of the pigs to get out of here. We don't want any within a mile. Second, we want a car with a police radio and a full tank of gas. And we want it delivered right out in front of the store."

"Okay," agreed Harry.

"When the street is clear, we'll take two hostages with us—the women. If anybody tries to stop us or follow us or interfere in any way, we'll blow their fucking heads off. Do I make myself clear?"

"Real clear."

The leader smiled with smug satisfaction. "Good. Now you get your ass out of here and do like I said. We'll give you exactly five minutes, sucker. After that we'll start tossing out a body every five minutes. And remember, you clowns try anything cute and they're dead."

Harry got up off the floor, the shotgun still leveled at his head. He started toward the door.

"Run, pig!" snarled the leader. "Before I shoot your pig ass off!" He suddenly kicked Harry in the butt with a tremendous boot that sent him sprawling onto the sidewalk.

Slowly Harry stood up, looking down at his good suit. It was a wreck.

"I said run, pig!"

Harry glanced back at the Chicano leader, who stood grinning in the doorway, then started to trot back toward the line of police cars at the end of the street.

"What's the deal?" the sergeant wanted to know when Harry ran up.

"We play it their way," breathed Harry. "Get these black-and-whites out of here."

"But Lieutenant Bressler said—"

"I don't care what Bressler said," snapped Harry. "We try to stall these punks, we're going to have bodies all over the street. They're not just playing games, they're dead serious. They'll kill those people. You want that?"

"No . . ."

"Then move your ass."

The sergeant looked at Harry uncertainly, then turned to the other uniformed policemen. "All right," he ordered, "you heard what the man said—get these cars out of here right now! Clear the area!"

After the sergeant moved off, DiGeorgio handed Harry his Magnum. "I don't think he likes you, Harry."

"Who does?" Harry returned.

As a young patrolman passed them on his way to a car, Harry grabbed the man's tear-gas gun, which he handed to DiGeorgio. "It's for you, fatso. I want you to cover me from the corner. When the action starts, I want you to fill that store with tear gas."

"What are you going to do?"

"Play it by ear." Harry clicked open the cylinder of the Magnum, making sure that all six chambers were loaded.

"Be careful somebody doesn't shove that ear up your ass," DiGeorgio warned.

"It's my ear and my ass."

One by one the patrol cars drove away, until finally only Harry's car was left. DiGeorgio moved off to the cover of a drugstore at the corner. Harry waited until DiGeorgio was in position, then climbed into the car. He slid the Magnum down into the slot between the seat cushion and the back, where it would not move easily, but also where it would be within quick reach.

27

Then, with a last glance at DiGeorgio, Harry started the car and drove down the street.

As the car approached the store, the Chicano leader appeared in the doorway, shotgun in hand. He waved for Harry to stop. Instead Harry jammed his foot down hard on the accelerator and spun the wheel. The car lurched forward and swerved right toward the store. Seeing what was happening, the leader raised his shotgun and fired off a blast. The shot took out the whole windshield, pulverizing it in a shower of glass. Harry ducked down behind the padded dashboard, still driving. The leader just had time to dive back into the store, out of the way, before the police car came smashing through the door and the brick wall and the window. Harry kept his foot on the accelerator. The car smashed into a display counter, taking out an entire row of expensive Sebastiani wines before it came to a final, jarring stop in the middle of the store.

Even before the car had stopped, Harry had the door open and was bringing the big Magnum up. It was chaotic inside the store. Hostages were screaming and running. As Harry climbed out of the car, the Chicano leader, who had been knocked down by the collapsing wall of bricks, was coming up, dragging his sawed-off shotgun out of the rubble that covered it. He and Harry saw each other at the same time. A fraction of a second before the leader could fire, Harry squeezed the trigger of the Magnum. The boom of the shot echoed through the store like an explosion. The bullet hit the leader in the chest, smashing him backwards like a rag doll. As the man went down, his shotgun went off, firing high and wide of Harry, ripping a hole in the ceiling. The leader rolled over, clutching his bloody chest, trying to get up, but unable to make it. He rolled back into the rubble and lay still.

Meanwhile the hostages were scrambling for safety, all except for the old black woman, who was still standing in the middle of the room.

"Behind you!" she shouted at Harry as he started to move toward her. Harry whirled to see the Chinese hood coming around the back fender of the car.

28

"Fucking pig sonofabitch!" he screamed, firing at Harry.

Harry felt part of the shotgun blast in his leg. He shot from the hip. The Chinese hood was hit in the thigh and went crashing back into a delicatessen case. Salami and cheese covered his body.

"There's one back there!" yelled the black woman, pointing at the back of the store.

"Get down, goddammit!" Harry shouted. She ducked behind an overturned bookrack.

At this moment DiGeorgio fired the tear-gas canister. It crashed onto the hood of the police car, bounced, and rattled across the floor into a corner, where it began to hiss. Thick white smoke began to fill the store.

Through the smoke Harry saw the pockmarked kid running for the back of the store, coughing furiously from the gas, his hand covering his mouth. He reached the back door and tried the knob. It was locked. He kicked at the door several times, finally managed to force it open, ran into the back storage room. Harry fired, hitting the kid right in the ass. The impact of the bullet sent him flying out of the back door, crashing through a row of cardboard boxes.

Three down and one to go, counted Harry. A cloud of white gas hit him right in the face. He winced and backed away from the cloud, his eyes filling with painful tears. He fought to keep his eyes open, looking around the store. Where the hell was the bastard hiding, anyway?

A movement near the door caught his attention. The last one, the Chicano with the broken nose, was edging toward the door, using a cashier's counter for cover. Harry ducked behind the police car and moved toward the door to head him off. The moment Harry came around the tail end of the car, Broken Nose spotted him, snapped up his thirty-eight, and blasted off a shot. Harry felt the bullet scream past his ear.

"Freeze, asshole!" Harry barked.

Broken Nose looked uncertainly at Harry, contemplating whether or not to give up. His look suddenly hardened, and he began to squeeze the trigger. Harry caught the flicker of movement and fired again. The bullet hit Broken Nose in the stomach, knocking him backwards through the open front door. He skidded across the pavement and slid to a stop against a red-white-and-blue mailbox. He did not move again.

Coughing and gasping, Harry stepped out of the store. Tear gas poured out into the street, drifting skywards. Harry looked down at the punk's body, hooked a foot under his shoulder, and kicked him over. He did not have to look closely to know he was dead. He had seen enough men killed to know the look of death.

Behind Harry the store owner came staggerinng out, a handkerchief clutched to his face, eyes red and wet from the gas. He was a short, balding man with thick glasses. He tugged the glasses off, wiped them clean, and stared incredulously at the ruins of his establishment.

"My store!" he cried, throwing up his hands in horror. "Who's going to pay for my store?"

Harry stared at the owner coldly, then nodded at the body on the pavement.

"Ask him."

Wearily Harry holstered the Magnum, looking down at his clothes. A wreck. His best suit, from the Emporium, completely ruined. A hundred and fifty-five dollars down the drain. And for what?

DiGeorgio came running down the street. "Hey, Harry," he cried breathlessly, "you okay?"

Harry smiled thinly. "Never felt better."

DiGeorgio looked at the store, the wrecked car, the bodies. He shook his head in astonishment. "Jesus Christ—why do you always have to do everything the hard way?"

Harry shrugged innocently. "What was hard about it?"

Three

The homicide squadroom was nearly deserted as Harry and DiGeorgio walked in. Only two of the twelve detectives' desks were occupied. Inspector Ken Chew was typing up a report, while his partner, Rich Anderson, hunched over his desk, talking to a sloppily dressed, overweight Italian woman. They seemed to be arguing about something. The woman's mouth was twisted into a frown. She shook her finger at Anderson, jabbing it toward his nose to underscore whatever point she was making. Anderson looked up briefly, saw Harry and DiGeorgio, and rolled his eyes in exasperation. Poor Rich, thought Harry, always getting stuck with the kooks.

While DiGeorgio hung up his coat, Harry crossed the room to a coffeepot on a corner table. The table stood next to an old, battered refrigerator. The homicide detectives often worked several days straight on a single case without a break, catching naps when they could, eating whatever was available. As a result the refrigerator was always stuffed with a variety of readily edible foods, including milk, sandwich meats, assorted cheeses, hard-boiled eggs, and an occasional apple pie made by Anderson's wife when she had the time.

After pouring himself a cup of coffee, Harry pulled open the refrigerator door. He selected a slice of bologna and a slice of American cheese. He slapped the two together, folded them over, and shoved them into his mouth, downing them in two bites. Among the members of the homicide squad, Harry Callahan's eating habits were almost as legendary as his prowess with a handgun. It was well known, for example, that he often ate cheese, bacon, and banana sandwiches, seemingly without ill effects. Another of his culinary favorites was a hamburger with peanut butter spread thickly on the top.

Chew stood up from his desk and ambled over, smiling knowingly at Harry. "Lieutenant Bressler's been looking for you," he said. "I'd say he sounds pissed off."

"He's always pissed off," replied Harry.

"In case you're interested, I think he's down at McKay's office right now."

Harry snorted. "I wonder what our glorious captain wants now. Probably needs somebody to scratch his ass for him. Between him and Bressler, they might even be able to figure out which hand to use."

Chew laughed. "Better not let McKay hear you say that."

"I'd write it out for him, but I don't think he's learned how to read."

"You've got a bad attitude, Harry," said Chew with mock severity. "It's guys like you that give this department a rotten reputation."

Harry forced a nasty look. "Keep it up, Chew, and I'll use your tongue for toilet paper."

Chew chuckled and went back to his typewriter. Harry carried his coffee cup over to his desk, where he plopped down in his chair. He looked at the wall clock. Six-thirty. Outside he could see the flickering lights of rush-hour traffic on Bryant Street moving toward the Bay Bridge, headed for Oakland and beyond. Somewhere, Harry thought enviously, somebody was sitting down right now to a nice home-cooked dinner made by a beautiful wife. After that they would go upstairs and make love for several hours. Somewhere. But not here. Here, Inspector Callahan is sitting on his can, looking out of the window, daydreaming like a jerk when he should be working. With a grunt of resignation Harry turned his attention to his desk.

Unlike the other detectives' desks, which were relatively neat, Harry's was a mess, covered with an array of reports, books, crumpled papers, and the like. He looked at one unfinished report about a heroin pusher arrested for the murder of his girl friend in North Beach. That arrest had been made two days ago, and still Harry had not gotten around to finishing the report. He knew if it wasn't in by tomorrow, Bressler would be crawling all over him again.

Harry picked up a clean police report form, wound it into his typewriter, and began to type hunt-and-peck. After over nineteen years of writing police reports, Harry still had not learned to type properly. Someday he would definitely have to learn, but for the moment it was simply not one of his priorities.

Almost immediately he made a mistake. With a muttered oath he grabbed an eraser and rubbed out the error, then went on typing. Of all the jobs that were a part of his regular routine, Harry hated typing the most.

He heard the door to the squad room bang open. Lieutenant Al Bressler stood in the doorway. He was a big shambling, pockmarked, red-faced man given to wearing expensive suits and loud, colorful ties. Such clothes should have made Bressler look like an insurance salesman, but they didn't. With that face and that build he looked like exactly what he was: an aging, harried, overworked cop.

Bressler's angry eyes swept the occupants of the room, resting finally on Harry with something less than warmth. Bressler's red face turned redder.

"Callahan!" The word exploded from Bressler's mouth like an accusation. "Where the hell have you been?"

"Getting laid," Harry said.

Bressler glared. "This is serious, Harry. Save the jokes for later."

DiGeorgio shot Harry a look of caution, then turned to Bressler. "We were at the hospital, Al, checking those punks who held up that liquor store, trying to get statements."

Bressler nodded, his eyes still locked on Harry. "Let's go, Callahan."

"Where to?"

"A little walk down the hall. Captain McKay wants to have a little chat with you. Personally." The words had an ominous ring to them.

Harry was surprised. McKay himself. The captain seldom lowered himself to talking personally to the men who worked homicide, allowing that chore to Bressler. Messages were generally relayed through the lieutenant. McKay was usually busy with more important things, such as attending city council luncheons or playing golf with the mayor. If McKay wanted to talk to Harry in his office, it had to be something big. And Harry was fairly certain he knew what it was.

Harry eased back his chair from the desk, took a final sip of coffee, then got to his feet. He followed Bressler down the hall, past the burglary detail squad room, to McKay's office at the end.

Ana Malave, McKay's pretty black secretary, nodded as they walked into the outer office. "Go on in. He's expecting you."

Bressler turned to Harry. "Look, Harry, behave yourself while you're in there. He's ready to go through the roof if you get sarcastic."

"I'm all broken up," said Harry solemnly.

"Come on. I'm just asking you to play it cool. For both our sakes."

Bressler opened the door and led the way inside. McKay's office was spacious, fancy, and comfortable, more like an executive's than a policeman's. The walls were decorated with various awards, commendations, and photographs, most notable of which was a large picture of McKay and the mayor taken at the Marin Golf and Country Club. Harry reacted with immediate distaste as he saw the photograph.

Bradford McKay was seated at his desk, a tough, cold, neat man in his late forties. Harry gazed at his superior with ill-concealed contempt. It wasn't really that he disliked the man personally, but rather that he hated the type he represented. As far as Harry was concerned, McKay was an ass-kisser, making friends with important people, playing politics, currying favor. He was an ambitious man with a single-minded determination to make it all the way to the top, willing to settle for nothing less. Someday McKay would probably make chief. He had enough friends in the right places. When he did, Harry would still dislike him just as intensely then as he did now.

Bressler closed the door.

"Sit down, Callahan," McKay said. It was an order, not a request. McKay seldom asked anyone to do anything.

Harry slid down into a chair in front of the big executive-type desk. Bressler, he noticed, remained standing by the door.

McKay leaned back in his chair, pressing the tips of his fingers together to form an arch. He looked like the president of General Motors about to address a board meeting. "I've just spent an hour in the chief's office upstairs," he began in a low voice. "Do you have any idea why, Callahan?"

Harry looked at McKay innocently. He hated playing question-and-answer games. Just get to the damned point, he thought. "He wanted your autograph?"

"Don't give me any of your crap," snapped McKay. The irritation in his voice was plain. "I'm not in the mood for it. I've spent a bad day, and I don't need much of an excuse to take you apart. If you give me a reason, I'll do it right now. With pleasure." He leaned forward accusingly, his face turning pink. "Do you know what the cost of that little circus you had this afternoon comes to in dollars and cents?"

Harry didn't know and didn't care. "Suppose you tell me."

McKay picked up a piece of paper, which he waved furiously. "Fourten thousand, three hundred and seventy-nine dollars; And that's not including personal

35

damages, which will probably come to a hell of a lot more."

Even Harry was surprised by the enormity of the figure. "How can that be?"

"You want an itemized account?" McKay referred to the paper. "In your outrageous efforts you took out two front doors, one front plate-glass window, twelve feet of brick wall, five display cases, three light fixtures, and a cash register. Plus damages to the stock, including forty-three bottles of wine, twenty-six bottles of imported champagne, sixteen bottles of Scotch, twenty-one bottles of bourbon, and eighteen bottles of assorted liqueurs. Plus one city police vehicle totally demolished, a nineteen seventy-four Impala. Not to mention three suspects in the hospital. All of whom will probably sue the city."

"What the hell for?"

McKay glowered at Harry. "Excessive use of force. My God, Callahan, where does it say in the rulebook that you've got a right to drive a car through the window of a store? You could have killed one of the hostages!"

"It seemed like the best thing to do at the time," Harry replied quietly. "Under the circumstances, I didn't have very many options."

"Lieutenant Bressler was on the way with a Tactical Squad. You knew that. The officer on the scene, Sergeant Wathen, told you. You should have waited until your superior arrived on the scene with the Tac Squad. They're specially trained to handle exactly that kind of situation, and you damned well know it!"

"In case you don't know it, those punks were about to start killing people. They had already shot a police officer, and he's still in the hospital in critical condition. They're not sure he's going to make it. I had exactly five minutes to decide what to do. By the time the Tac Squad got there, the whole thing was over. What was I supposed to do, let those bastards start throwing bodies out into the street?"

McKay pursed his lips and regained his poise. "You should have stalled them along."

Harry's voice was filled with contempt. "You tell me how to stall four guys armed with shotguns and thirty-eights. I don't sing and dance very well, and I couldn't think of any funny stories to tell. Maybe I should have started throwing water balloons at them."

McKay was furious with Harry's sarcastic attitude. He fought to control his anger, turning away to Bressler. "Did you get those hospital reports on the wounded suspects yet?"

"Frank and I were just over there," Harry cut in before Bressler could answer. "One of them was D.O.A. The rest will live."

"Where were they hit?"

"One in the chest. One in the ass."

"What about the other one?"

Harry smiled slightly. "Let's just say he'll be singing soprano for a while."

"You seem to think all of this is amusing, Callahan." McKay stood up and came around the front of his desk. He sat on the edge, staring down at Harry with cold dislike.

"Not all of it."

"For your information, the minority community of this city has just about had it with this kind of police work. It's downright disgraceful."

Harry frowned. "By minority community I take it you mean the hoods?"

"It so happens they're American citizens, too. They happen to have rights."

"So does that old lady who had a sawed-off shotgun sticking in her ear. Or doesn't she count any more? What the hell is going on around here? What kind of department are we running where we're more concerned with the rights of the criminals than of the people we're supposed to be protecting? It seems to me we've got our priorities ass-backwards."

"Your job is to uphold the laws, Callahan, not simply break them whenever you get the urge to go out and play cowboy. You're not Wild Bill Hickok. You're a policeman—or at least that's what you're supposed to be. You've got a responsibility to this city and to this department to act responsibly. If every man on this force acted the way you do, we'd all be out of our jobs within a week, trying to collect unemployment."

"If everybody on this force did what I do," returned Harry acidly, "the streets would be a lot safer than they are now. How do you expect to lower the crime rate when every time I pull my gun out, some candy-ass up on top gets hysterical and breaks out in hives?"

"Every time I turn around you're in trouble, Callahan. This isn't the first time you've had your ass in the fire. Last year you beat up that sixteen-year-old kid so bad he had to be put in intensive care."

"That sixteen-year-old choirboy you're so concerned about had a submachine gun," Harry pointed out. "Besides, the way I see it he was lucky."

"And just how do you figure that one? He had a broken arm, fractured ribs, a broken nose, and a concussion."

"Yeah. But I could have killed him."

McKay favored Harry with a look that suggested he was stark raving mad. "Before that," he went on, "it was that thing with that sniper, Scorpio. You broke every rule in the book on that one and damned near lost your job. You get into one mess after another, dragging the department along with you. When are you going to learn that being a cop doesn't give you an excuse to go around acting like a goddamn stuntman?"

"I'm just doing my job," said Harry coolly.

"You're hopeless," snapped McKay. "As a result of your childish stupidity, the press is crying police brutality—"

"What else is new?"

"—and the city council is up in arms! There's an election coming up here in a few months. Every politician in the city is looking for a cause to jump on so he can make a few points with the voters out there. And now you've given them one of a silver platter."

"I'm not a politician, just a cop."

McKay opened a mahogany humidor on his desk

and selected a cigar from it. Harry noted, without surprise, that he did not offer one to anyone else.

"I'm not about to debate this with you, Inspector Callahan. I've been on the phone with the mayor twice this morning, and I'll tell you he went right through the ceiling over this one. If anything, he's even madder about this than the chief is. If there's one thing he doesn't need so close to elections, it's a hot little issue like police brutality." McKay struck a match, which he held to the end of the cigar.

Harry waited until the cigar was lit, then said, "Did you tell him about the meeting?"

"What meeting?"

"Here. In this office. Two months ago. When you said that the mayor wanted the number-one priority of this department to be running the hoods and the scum out of San Francisco. You said you wanted safer streets, a city where people could walk at night without being afraid. You remember that little talk we had now, Captain?"

"I never said use violence," insisted McKay through a cloud of smoke.

"Oh, I see. What are we supposed to do, then? Jump out from behind a lamppost and go 'Boo'?"

"All right now, Harry," said Bressler, speaking up for the first time since they had entered the room, "I think that's just about enough."

"How about 'Trick or treat'?" Harry went on, ignoring Bressler. "Maybe we could even slap their hands in extreme cases. Lightly, of course, because we wouldn't want to get violent. That might upset the mayor. And we sure wouldn't want that. Would we, Captain?"

McKay flicked his cigar over a bronze ashtray. "I'll say this just once. I expect you and every other man on this force to behave with restraint . . . or turn in his resignation." McKay paused, letting the last remark sink in. "As of right now, you're on notice, Callahan. That little Wild West show of yours is exactly the kind of thing that this department is no longer prepared to tolerate. Is that clear?"

McKay waited for an answer, but Harry said nothing. At last Bressler spoke up for him. "Yes sir. He understands, sir."

"Well, if that's all, Captain," said Harry with exaggerated politeness, "I'll be going. I'd really like to stick around a while longer, but I've got work to do."

McKay smiled smugly. "But not in homicide."

"What does that mean?"

"I told you I talked to the chief. We both agreed that as of this moment, you're off homicide. For the time being you've been transferred to Personnel."

Harry stiffened. "Personnel!" He almost spit the word out.

"That's it," nodded McKay. He was, Harry could see, enjoying this. This was the moment he had been waiting for. The rest of it had just been a buildup. "You report tomorrow morning to the Oral Examining Board at nine o'clock. They're examining applicants for the grade of inspector. The chief and I feel that a man of your . . . ah . . . experience should be invaluable there."

Harry stood up, eyeing McKay coldly. "Congratulations, Captain. You finally got your way, didn't you?"

"What way is that?"

"Getting me off homicide. That's exactly what you've wanted for months." He flashed a vicious smile. "Okay for now. But I wouldn't get too comfortable if I were you. I'll be back."

"Not if I can help it," replied McKay.

Harry stared at his superior for a moment, then turned and stalked out of the office.

Four

At nine-thirty the next morning Harry drove his racing green Corvette into the Hall of Justice parking lot, screeched around a black-and-white blocking his way, and slid into his reserved space with practiced ease. He glanced at his watch, grunting disgustedly. His first day on the job and he was already a half-hour late. That should really make him popular with the Personnel Board. Well, to hell with them. If they wanted his badge so much, they could have it. He wasn't going to worry about it. He hadn't wanted this job in the first place—that had been McKay's brilliant idea.

Harry clambered out, locked the car door, and slammed it. He headed for the side entrance at a brisk pace. The thought of McKay gloating about his transfer renewed Harry's anger from the day before. Why was it always bastards like that who made it to the top? The ones who had no real knowledge of what it took to be a cop? McKay had never, as far as Harry knew, spent a day out on the street. He was what was known as a "desk cop" among the other officers. His appointment to captain two years ago had been purely political, based not on his experience, but on his influence with the right people. It was galling that a man like that should get an important promotion while other men with better qualifications were passed over. But those were the breaks. Maybe it was just as well that McKay was behind a desk, rather than out on the street someplace screwing things up where it really counted. The idea of McKay with a gun was frightening when you thought about it. Harry wondered how long it had been since McKay had qualified with his revolver. The chances were, like most of the top brass, he couldn't hit a damned thing.

At the end of the basement hall Harry entered the elevator. As he stepped out on the third floor he saw a group of hookers being herded into a courtroom by two officers.

"Hey, Harry, what's happening, baby?"

One of the hookers was beaming at Harry. She was black, closing in on forty, but still attractive for her age, considering the rigors of her profession. She was wearing an outrageous pink hotpants suit and too much makeup.

"How are you, Jenny?" Harry asked with a friendly grin. She had been a witness once, several years ago, in a murder case involving a teen-age boy.

The hooker jerked up one shoulder in a shrug. "Aw, you know how it is, honey. The same old thing. What else would I be doing?"

"Thought you would have retired by now."

"Honey, somebody's got to pay the bills."

Harry laughed, continuing on down the hall.

"Come on by for a free sample sometime!" she called after him.

"I don't have the back for it," Harry returned.

The hookers cackled hysterically.

The Oral Board Room was near the end of the hall. There were about fifteen officers sitting in a line of chairs along the wall. Four of them, Harry noticed, were women. It was something that he still had not resigned himself to: female police. Not that Harry considered himself a chauvinist. While he did not like most feminists, he did believe in equal rights for both sexes. But he had been a police officer for a long time, and he had no illusions about how demanding and dangerous the job was. Harry simply did not think most women were up to the job physically. For that matter, few men were.

Inside the board room four people were seated at a long, plain conference table. Harry immediately recognized Lieutenant Charles Dobbs, an officer he had had disagreements with more than once, and Inspector Mike Kraus. Dobbs was animatedly talking to a young officer seated across from him, a man Harry had seen before but did not know very well. Thompson or Thomas or something like that. Harry did not know the fourth person at all, a prim, middle-aged woman with a face that drew in upon itself in tight wrinkles.

"Okay," Dobbs was saying to the young policeman, "now here's the situation. I'm the robber, you're the cop. Right? I'm standing in a supermarket, and you've just caught me dead bang in the middle of a two-eleven." Dobbs was so deeply into his little dramatic improvisation that he did not notice Harry standing in the doorway watching him, smiling. "You order me to throw down my gun and put up my hands. But instead of doing that I grab a hostage, an eleven-year-old kid who just happens to be standing within easy reach. There's no time for you to call for assistance. I've got the kid, I've got a gun, and I'm going to blow the kid's head off. There's no way you're going to take me alive. Here I come—you've got ten seconds to make up your mind. What are you going to do?" Dobbs came around the table, holding an imaginary gun in one hand and the invisible kid with the other. "Come on now," he demanded. "Ten seconds. One . . . two . . . three . . ."

The young policeman was paralyzed, swept up in the situation, with absolutely no idea what he should do. He just sat there looking blankly at Dobbs, his eyes as big as saucers. This was beyond anything he had been prepared for.

Dobbs slowly moved in on the young man, who in turn slowly backed away.

"Four . . . five . . . do something, goddammit! Don't just stand there! I'm going to kill the kid! Seven . . . eight . . ."

The young cop continued to sit there, frozen to the spot. He opened his mouth, but was unable to speak. His fingers began to twitch in absolute terror.

At this point Harry made a gun with his thumb and forefinger, which he leveled at Dobbs's head. "Bang, you're dead!"

Dobbs whirled around, startled, still holding his imaginary gun and hostage. He glared at Harry, dropping his hands. "You're half an hour late, Inspector Callahan! We start here at nine o'clock sharp! Weren't you aware of that?"

"I got delayed in traffic," said Harry affably. "There's a big accident on Mission. You're lucky I got here at all." He nodded at Inspector Kraus. "Hey, Mike, how you doing?."

Kraus kicked back in his chair. "I'm kinda surprised to see you here, Harry. Don't tell me you got tired of working homicide?"

"It was the other way around, I'm afraid. Homicide got tired of me."

"You mean McKay finally got tired of your crap and tossed you out?"

"Temporarily," Harry admitted. "He was just jealous of my growing popularity."

Kraus chuckled. "Sure. You're about as popular as diarrhea, Harry."

"All right, Thompson," Dobbs told the young officer, "you can go now. You'll be notified of your grade." His voice held little promise.

"Sorry, Lieutenant," Thompson apologized. "I just sort of froze up there for a moment. It won't happen again."

"Suppose you just sort of froze up during the real thing?" asked Harry curtly. "You'd get a lot of people killed and probably yourself along with them."

Thompson lowered his eyes as he left.

Dobbs turned to face Harry again. "From now on, Callahan, I expect you to be here on time. We've got ourselves a heavy schedule. There are fifty officers to be tested."

"For how many vacancies?"

"Eight. There will be five men and three women promoted to the rank of inspector out of this group."

"Three women promoted to inspector?" asked Harry in surprise. "You've got to be kidding!"

"We're not kidding," interjected the middle-aged woman sharply. "I take it you object to the idea of women being promoted to that rank?"

"This is Ms. Grey of the mayor's staff," explained Dobbs. "She's been assigned to monitor these examinations."

"The mayor's staff?"

"That's right," said Ms. Grey with cold pride.

"Figures," commented Harry.

Dobbs gave Harry a warning look, then said, "Ms. Grey, this is Detective Inspector Harry Callahan. He's just been transferred to personnel from homicide."

Ms. Grey nodded. "Yes, I've heard of Inspector Callahan." Her tone of voice told Harry that what she had heard had not been very good.

"I'll just bet you have."

"Let me make it quite clear to you, Inspector, that it is the mayor's intention that this department be brought more into line with the mainstream of twentieth-century thinking."

Harry forced a smile. "I see. And just how does he figure to do that?"

"For one thing," replied Ms. Grey briskly, "His Honor intends to broaden the areas of participation for women within the structure of the police force. Times have changed, Inspector, although I'm sure you haven't noticed. Women are no longer second-class citizens in this society. They have been liberated. They are an equal part of our culture, and they will have equal jobs. The City of San Francisco is going to set new standards for the rest of the country."

"That sounds very stylish," said Harry. He did not sound at all enthusiastic.

Ms. Grey gave Harry an acid look. "I believe he also said something about winnowing the neanderthals out of the department."

"That sounds like something he'd say, all right," noted Harry sourly.

Dobbs cleared his throat loudly. "We're a little bit

pushed for time, due to your tardiness, Callahan. So why don't we just table this conversation for the moment and get on with the job at hand." He crossed to the door and leaned out, calling, "Next applicant!"

A woman in uniform came through the door. She was mildly attractive, in a kind of stiff fashion, and she had nice legs, Harry noticed, from what he could see where he was sitting. He caught himself smiling appreciatively and immediately forced a scowl.

Dobbs consulted a sheet of paper. "Officer Kathryn Moore?"

"Yes, sir."

"Sit down, please."

Officer Moore sat. Dobbs and Harry both took their chairs behind the long table.

"As you know," began Dobbs, "this is the final stage in your examination. It's a rather informal test in which we try to get some line on your ability to think on your feet, your reaction to stress and pressures, your ability to apply the law in a hypothetical situation, and so on. Try not to be nervous. We're not here to crucify you. Consider us your friends."

"Yes, sir."

"How long have you been on the force?"

"Nine years."

"What department?"

"Mainly Personnel and Records."

At the last answer Harry sniffed audibly.

"Something wrong with that, Callahan?" questioned Dobbs.

"That depends."

"On what?"

Harry folded his hands in front of him. "Seems to me that it would be more practical if she'd had some field experience."

"She has to begin somewhere," put in Ms. Grey.

Harry looked over at the woman from the mayor's office. "This is a police department, not a vocational training school. We need trained people who know what the hell they're doing."

46

"Callahan," said Dobbs firmly, "do you have any questions for the applicant?"

"Questions?" Harry's face was blank. "Uh . . . yeah. Questions. Let's see." He frowned in thought. "Here's one. How fast do you do the hundred?"

"Come on, Callahan," growled Dobbs impatiently. "Stop playing around. You know how this board functions."

"Sorry." Harry got up and crossed to the water cooler. As he filled a paper cup, he said, "All right, Officer Moore, let me ask you this. You understand, don't you, that if you make inspector, under the mayor's new guidelines, you'll probably end up in a police car?"

Officer Moore nodded. "Yes. That's what I'm hoping for."

"I see." Harry drained his cup and filled it again. "Well, then, why don't you tell us about your most important felony arrest?"

"I've never made a felony arrest."

"Well, tell us about your best misdemeanor arrest."

Officer Moore shifted her weight uncomfortably in her chair. She took a small breath. "To tell you the truth, I've never made a misdemeanor arrest, either."

"So what the hell makes you think you're qualified to ride in a police car when you've never made a single arrest and there are patrolmen out there with ten or fifteen years of experience in the street?" Harry crumpled up the cup and tossed it in the trash.

Ms. Grey was bristling. "The woman's place is in the home, is that what you're trying to say, Inspector Callahan? Women have no business in a man's world?"

Harry whirled. "I'm just trying to be intelligent. What the hell do you think it's like out there, lady? It's a tough world, not some encounter group."

"I don't think I like the tone of your voice," replied Ms. Grey stiffly.

"Well, I'd like to know what happens to this officer when some crazy bastard sticks a gun in her face and yells, *'Hit the deck, you dirty bitch, before I blow your fucking head off!'* What happens then?"

47

Ms. Grey leaned forward in her chair, her eyes wide with anger. "You're just deliberately trying to fail this candidate, aren't you?"

"You're goddamn right," Harry agreed. "If she fails in here, she'll just go back to Personnel, and that's all. But if she fails out there, she's liable to get her cute little ass blown off."

"Well," said Officer Moore in a tone that matched his, "it's my ass—and my hard luck."

"Not exactly," replied Harry. "Because you won't be alone out there. You'll have a partner who will be counting on you. If you do screw up and get yourself blown away, the chances are that he'll get blown away with you. We'll have two dead officers and God only knows how many civilians. And that's one hell of a goddamn price to pay just so our mayor can tell everybody he's stylish."

Harry and Officer Moore glared at each other, neither liking the other one bit. This did not bother Harry at all. He was used to not being liked by people, and he himself seldom liked anybody else.

Finally Dobbs spoke up to break the cold silence that had fallen over the room. "Are you finished with your questions, Callahan? We're in a bit of a hurry—"

"Not quite." Harry stood up. "I've got one more, if it's all right with you."

"Go ahead. But make it brief."

Harry leaned forward, studying Officer Moore with a serious look. "I've got a hypothetical situation, okay?"

She looked across at him supiciously, straightening her skirt self-consciously. "What is it?"

"Let's say I'm standing on a street corner minding my own business, sucking my thumb or whatever, when Missus Grey here comes up and propositions me, okay?" Harry glanced around and saw that Ms. Grey was turning red. He waited for her protest, but she said nothing. He went on. "She wants me to go over to her place where for five dollars she will put on an exhibition with a Shetland pony."

This was too much for Ms. Grey. She jumped to her feet furiously. "If this is your idea of humor—"

"What are you trying to do here?" yelled Dobbs.

Harry watched them both calmly. "I'm trying to find out if anybody in this room knows what the hell law is being broken in that situation—" he glanced at Ms. Grey's portly figure—"besides cruelty to animals."

Officer Moore spoke up quickly. "For your information, Inspector, that's a conspiracy under title seven, section one eighty-two, paragraph one of the California State Penal Code."

Harry was surprised by her answer, and somewhat chagrined. "Uh . . . yeah. Okay, fine."

But Officer Moore was not finished. "According to the People versus Bashore, nineteen sixty-five," she plunged on, "a conspiracy to commit a misdemeanor is, in fact, a felony, and is punishable by not more than three years in a state prison or a five-hundred-dollar fine. Or both." She looked at Harry with a definite smirk.

Order returned to the room. Ms. Grey sat back down, somewhat stiffly, and fixed Harry with an icy stare. Dobbs, as surprised as Harry by Officer Moore's answer, smiled at her.

"Excellent answer," Dobbs said. "You've obviously done your homework and know your lawbooks. Good work. I think that will be all for now. Thank you. You'll be notified of your grade in a day or so."

Officer Moore picked up her handbag and, with one final, triumphant look at Harry, left.

When the door closed behind her, Dobbs turned to the others. "Well, what do you think?"

Harry bit his lower lip. "I think it's a hell of a way to run a police force."

At lunchtime Harry ran into Frank DiGeorgio in the police cafeteria, sitting at a table by himself, wolfing down a plateful of spaghetti.

"How's it it going, Harry?" asked DiGeorgio, mouth full of food.

Harry put down his tray and sat glaring at his

plate. "Spent the whole goddamn morning talking to a bunch of half-assed morons who want to make inspector. Every one of them thinks he's the Blue Knight. And not one of them has any idea what the hell he's doing. The Academy graduates get worse and worse every damned year. God only knows what's going to happen in the future." He opened a paper carton of milk, which he poured into a plastic glass. Then he crumpled the carton and dropped it back on his tray. "They don't even know which way to point their guns, Frank. And you know what's even worse? You won't believe it, but they're going to promote three women along with the rest of them, just so the mayor can be stylish."

"No kidding? I think I heard something about that. Any of them good-looking?"

Harry looked pained. "They're all dogs with hairy legs and fat butts from sitting down all day twirling pencils. Women inspectors! I tell you, Frank, this whole department is going downhill so fast it makes knots in my stomach. If I had any sense at all I'd quit today and go get myself a job parking cars or pumping gas or something that makes more sense." He picked at his food without any real interest.

DiGeorgio laughed. "Fat chance. You wouldn't know how to do anything else. You've been a cop too long, Harry."

Harry picked up a bottle of ketchup, squirting the contents liberally on his hamburger. He slapped the top of the bun on and took an enormous bite. "What about you, fatso? They give you a new partner yet?"

"Ralph Chamberlain."

"Yeah? He's a good man. What cases they got you guys working on?"

"Usual stuff. Some pusher got his head blown off with a forty-five last night. They found his body in Golden Gate Park. The lab boys had to dig pieces of his skull out of a tree. Looks like it was his girl friend. He was getting pretty frisky with a couple other broads on the side, and she was the jealous type. Same old story."

50

Ketchup dribbled down Harry's chin. He wiped at it with his index finger. "Don't worry, I'll be back in homicide pretty soon."

"Who's worried? You really think McKay will ever let you near homicide again?"

"Sure. Just wait and see. Some big case'll come along that nobody else can handle, and they'll get desperate and tap me for it."

"You're so modest, Harry."

Harry shrugged. "Face it, Frank," he said seriously. "We all know I'm the best."

DiGeorgio raised his eyebrows. He carefully wound a strand of spaghetti around his fork. "Three women for inspector, huh?"

"Yeah. Isn't that the stupidest thing you've heard all week?"

"I wonder if any of them will end up in homicide."

"Christ," muttered Harry, "that's all we need."

Five

It was almost midnight. In a dark alley between two warehouses in San Francisco's waterfront district, a Western Gas and Electric Company truck was parked. The driver of the truck, Bobby Maxwell, sat calmly waiting. Far away he could hear the sound of a fog-horn blaring its mournful warning to ships in the bay.

Bobby checked his wristwatch. "Almost time," he said in a low voice.

He pivoted in his seat and looked at the six people seated on the floor in the back of the truck. His followers. His army. There was Miki, the blond hooker who had helped steal the truck. Lalo, a tough Chicano Bobby had known in Vietnam. Tex, a skinny redhead who had been a fellow inmate at San Quentin for two years. Wanda, a tall brunette, like Miki one of Bobby's hookers. Henry Lee Caldwell, a mean black dude, also a friend from 'Nam. And Karl, the hulking giant who almost never spoke, who could snap a man's spine with his bare hands as if it were a stick of wood. All of them tough, all of them ruthless, all of them willing to do whatever he told them. They would, Bobby knew, follow him into hell without a moment's hesitation.

"All right," he said, "let's go over it again. After I take care of the guard and get his keys, we drive to the far end of warehouse Fifty-A. Lalo?"

The Chicano looked up, eyes gleaming in the darkness. "I drop you off, then drive to the first big door on the wharf side. You open the door, and I back the truck around to the loading dock."

"Right," agreed Bobby. "Karl and Tex?"

"We grab the AR-15 automatic rifles," said Tex. "The heavy stuff.'

Karl nodded wordlessly.

Bobby turned his eyes to the two women. "Wanda?"

"Locate and take any explosives. Dynamite, detonators—and plastic explosives if they've got them."

"Miki?"

"You and I get the LAWS rockets. They should be somewhere at the back of the warehouse."

"Check." Bobby looked last at the black man. "Henry Lee?"

"I get the ammo for the automatic rifles—boss man."

Bobby grinned. "Beautiful. As long as everybody remembers his own gig, it'll go like clockwork." He checked his watch again. "Okay, time to go folks." He turned the key in the ignition. The truck rumbled to life.

Lalo stood up and came forward to sit in the passenger seat.

"One thing," Bobby reminded the others. "If anything goes wrong—no shooting if we can help it. Gunshots will bring the pigs down on us so fast it'll make you pee in your pants."

"Yeah," said Lalo, "but what if something does go wrong?"

Bobby grinned. He reached down into his boot and pulled something out. The long blade of his commando knife gleamed in his hand. "I'll handle it—with this!"

Inside the guardhouse at Pier Fifty, a fat, balding guard called Pop Siegel sat comfortably in his chair, listening to the radio and looking at a *Penthouse* centerfold.

It was a soft job, and Siegel liked it. It was warm, there was always a pot of hot coffee and a radio, and there was absolutely nothing to do from ten p.m. until six a.m., when the morning man came on duty.

Siegel eased back in his chair and looked again

at the *Penthouse* centerfold in front of him. Good God almighty! Look at the size of those knockers! They had to be thirty-eights or forties. Like watermelons. How did a woman built like that walk around without falling over forward? Imagine having stuff like that to come home to every night. Now, that would be something. He tried to let his imagination wander with the idea, but his thoughts kept coming back to his own wife, Nancy. At fifty-eight, Nancy Siegel was overweight, gray-haired, and frowzy. They still had sex occasionally, but not very often. Once every couple months, maybe. After twenty-five years of marriage there were few, if any, surprises left.

Siegel looked up from his magazine and gazed through the window of the guardhouse at Mission Rock Street. He was surprised to see headlights approaching out of the darkness. There was never much traffic at this time of night, not down here in China Basin. Usually the only traffic was a regular prowl car once every hour and an occasional teen-age kid looking for someplace to park his car so he could get his girl-friend in the back seat.

Siegel watched the headlights slow at the gate and stop. The driver honked. Siegel swore under his breath, put down the magazine, and went outside. A blast of cold air hit him in the face, wind from the Pacific whipping through the mouth of the bay.

"Hey, guard!" a voice called from behind the headlights. "Open up;"

Siegel zipped up the front of his bulky guard's jacket and unclipped his flashlight. He played it on the vehicle parked outside the gate. A utility truck. On the side he saw the words *Western Gas and Electric*.

He opened the gate enough to slip through, wondering what the hell the electric company wanted at this time of night. He hoped that, whatever, it was, they would make it quick so he could get back into his warm guardhouse.

"Hi there," said the driver amiably.

Siegel flashed the light on the driver's face. A young man in a gas company uniform. He had long hair and intense eyes. Siegel panned the flashlight to the face of the man beside the driver. A Mexican with long hair and a drooping mustache. A couple of hippies. How the hell did they get jobs, anyway? They shouldn't be allowed to work without cutting their hair. It was a goddamn disgrace, that's what it was. The damn hippies and minorities were taking over the whole country. It didn't matter if you were decent and clean-cut any more. The values of the country were going to hell.

"What is it?" asked Siegel. His voice betrayed his annoyance.

The driver fished around inside his jacket and pulled out an identification card. "Gas company."

Siegel didn't bother to look at the card. "What's the trouble?"

"There's a major gas leak in the area. Pipes busted somewhere. We've got to check out your underground layout. There's a manhole on your property some-where."

"That's right." Siegel jerked his head in the direction of one of the big warehouses. "Back there."

"We're going have to pull it and have a look in it."

Siegel groaned internally. He would have to keep an eye on them, and that meant standing out in the cold. "How long you figure it will take?"

"Hard to say," replied the driver. "We'll make it as fast as possible."

Siegel reached for his keys and unlocked the gates.

"And for Pete's sake, don't smoke," added the driver. "Not until I tell you it's okay."

"I won't, I won't." Siegel swung open the big gates.

"If it's seeping down into your sewer system, this whole damned block could explode."

The gates open, the driver started the truck, pulled through, and stopped. "Mind if I use your phone for a minute?" he asked, opening the cab door.

"Yeah, sure," said Siegel. "Right this way." He led the way into the guardhouse. He was just starting to tell the driver he had to dial nine to get an outside line when he felt a powerful hand clamp over his mouth.

56

Siegel struggled to pull away, saw a flash of steel, and felt the point of the knife pierce the bulky padding of his jacket. Oh God, he thought in that last split second, I'm going to die. And then he did die.

Bobby lowered the body to the floor, frisking the guard's pockets expertly. In a few moments he had found what he was looking for: the keyring.

He hurried out to the waiting truck. Lalo had moved behind the wheel and was shifting into gear. Bobby jumped in on the passenger side.

"Let's go!"

With a screech of rubber the vehicle roared off toward the line of warehouses. Lalo drove straight to warehouse Fifty-A. He slowed in front of an office door, and Bobby jumped out, unlocked the door, and disappeared inside. Lalo backed the truck around in a sharp half-circle and eased it up to the warehouse loading dock.

"Okay," Lalo told the others.

The back doors of the truck opened, and the commando group emerged. Bobby disappeared back into the dark warehouse. Moments later two rows of conical overhead lights came on, illuminating the area of the warehouse nearest the door. Wooden crates were stacked in long lines all the way to the back wall.

Bobby looked at his followers. "Come on, everybody!" he snapped. "Let's haul ass! We're on a time schedule!"

Frank DiGeorgio had a stomachache from eating too many chili dogs. He grunted as Ralph Chamberlain turned the unmarked police car onto Third Street and headed toward the China Basin warehouse district.

"You want to stop and get an Alka-Seltzer?" asked Chamberlain.

"Naw, that's okay," said DiGeorgio. "It's not so bad." He put a hand to his fat stomach and held it there. It wasn't really the stomach that bothered him so much as the fact that Harry Callahan was not sitting next to him. He and Harry had been friends for more years than either of them cared to remember. Not just working partners, but good buddies. They went fishing together, sometimes camping together. When DiGeorgio's wife, Irene, finally talked him into buying that old house on Noriega, it was Harry who had come over weekends and helped fix it up. Before Harry's wife had been killed in an automobile accident, the four of them often went to the races together on weekends. DiGeorgio and Irene, Harry and Louise. They had had lots of good times together. After Louise died, Harry seemed to change. He was colder, more distant. But they were still friends. Through all the times Harry had, been called on the carpet, they had remained so. And more than once, DiGeorgio knew, Harry had saved his ass in a tight situation.

DiGeorgio looked over at Ralph Chamberlain. A good cop who knew his stuff. Nine years on the force, two in homicide. A partner you could count on, sure. But he still missed Harry.

At the next intersection the car slowed. Chamberlain turned right onto Mission Rock Street. They swept past lines of dark warehouses, approaching Pier Fifty.

"That's funny," muttered Chamberlain.

DiGeorgio snapped out of his reverie. "What's funny?"

Chamberlain was staring off into the darkness. "The gates to Pier Fifty are standing open."

DiGeorgio looked. They sure as hell were—wide open. "Nobody in the guardhouse, either," he added. "We better check it out."

Chamberlain accelerated through the open gate. He pulled to a halt in front of the guardhouse. DiGeorgio got out and went inside. Pop Siegel's body was lying on the floor, face up, a large red stain covering his chest.

DiGeorgio swallowed. He looked back at the police car. "Ralph?"

Chamberlain came in and saw the body. "Oh, Jesus, poor Pop. He only had about six months left to retirement."

"He'll never get it now." said DiGeorgio. "Looks like somebody knifed him."

"Goddammit to hell."

DiGeorgio glanced out of the window at the ware-houses. He could see nothing moving. "You better call in for a backup. And an ambulance."

Chamberlain headed for the door. "Okay."

DiGeorgio followed him out, reaching inside his coat for his police issue three-fifty-seven Magnum. "I'm going to have a look-see around."

"Be careful," advised Chamberlain. "They already killed a guard, they won't hesitate on a cop."

"Yeah."

Inside the cab of the gas company utility truck, Lalo was beginning to get nervous. "Come on," he muttered to no one but himself, "let's move it." He reached into his pocket for a pack of cigarettes, then thought better of it. There were *No Smoking* signs all around. With all the ammunition and explosives around, lighting a cigarette would not be a very good idea. Instead he began to crack his knuckles, popping them one by one, just to give his hands something to do.

In the warehouse everything was going like clock-work. While the others took care of their specified jobs, Bobby and Miki located a cluster of crates against the back wall. Bobby hooked a crowbar under the lid of one crate and pried it up. The crate contained olive green fiberglass tubes three inches wide by about three and a half feet long. LAWS rockets—LAWS meaning Light Anti-tank Weapons System. Bobby grinned as he saw them; he was well acquainted with their use from his days in Vietnam. One-shot, disposable ba-zookas, capable of punching a hole in three-quarter-inch armored plate.

Bobby could barely contain his glee. All this stuff— the LAWS rockets, the automatic rifles, the explosives —was fantastic. With it they would be better equipped than the police were. They would be an army. An army the likes of which America had never seen. They would turn the city into a battleground. They would make the Watts riots look like a Sunday school picnic. The pigs, the mayor, the fat cats on top—all of them would be scared shitless before he was through. And he would be rich to boot. Far fucking out!

"This is it," Bobby told Miki. He rammed the lid back into place. He and Miki each carried a crate to the back of the waiting truck.

"Hey, Bobby!" It was Lalo, getting out of the truck, coming into the warehouse.

"What?"

"I thought I heard some noise up toward the gate. Sounded like a car."

Bobby looked at the others. They were nearly finished. "Okay," he said, "you help Miki with the rest of the LAWS. I'll go take a look."

"Okay."

Bobby's hand fell automatically to the hilt of his knife as he went through the door. He started down the long line of warehouses toward the main gate, which was just out of sight beyond the last warehouse. Then he froze suddenly, listening. He could hear the sound of approaching footsteps. Someone on tiptoes, trying to be quiet.

Quickly, Bobby ducked into the shadows of a narrow alley between two warehouses. Moments later Di-Georgio went past, gun in hand. Bobby sized up the fat man in the baggy gray suit for exactly what he was: a cop. He reached down, pulling the knife soundlessly out of its scabbard.

Just past the alley DiGeorgio pulled back into a doorway and watched the utility truck being loaded. Six people, four men and two women, were moving back and forth, carrying large wooden crates from the warehouse to the back of the truck. He waited until all six were visible, then moved out of the doorway into the light, gun held high.

"All right—hold it right there!"

The people with the crates froze in mid-step. DiGeorgio moved closer to cover them better.

"Now put down those boxes real slow."

The six did as they were told.

"Get your hands up where I can see them. And no sudden movements, or somebody's liable to get shot."

Again the six complied with DiGeorgio's orders.

"Listen, buddy," said Lalo calmly, "you're making a very big mistake. I don't know who you are or what this is all about, but we've got orders to pick this stuff up."

DiGeorgio nodded back in the direction of the gate. "There's a dead guard back there with a hole in his chest. Did you have orders to do that, too?"

Behind DiGeorgio, Lalo saw Bobby coming out of the shadows, creeping forward, knife held high. "I don't know anything about any guard, man." Lalo started to lower his hands.

"Stand still, I'm telling you!" barked DiGeorgio. "Make one more move and I'll mail you home to mama in a long box." He waved the barrel of the gun. "Against the wall now—all of you!"

Behind him DiGeorgio heard a noise. He whirled around, saw Bobby's knife coming down at him, and tried to block it with his arm. But the defensive move was too slow, and DiGeorgio felt the knife stab down into his shoulder. DiGeorgio cried out sharply, the three-fifty-seven Magnum going off. He saw the bullet hit one of the girls—she fell—and then Bobby stabbed him again, this time in the chest. DiGeorgio started to fall, the gun dropping from his hand. Again the knife came down, again sinking deep in his chest. He was covered with blood, falling, losing consciousness . . .

"Bobby—it's Miki—she's been shot!"

Bobby, staring down at DiGeorgio's body, saw the detective's chest rising and falling. He was still alive. Bobby raised the knife again for one more strike.

It was Lalo's voice. Bobby looked around and saw Lalo kneeling by Miki near the truck. He glanced back at DiGeorgio. Fuck it, the guy would be dead in five minutes anyhow. He ran over to where Miki had fallen.

"She's been shot in the stomach," said Lalo. "It looks real bad." He took her arms. "Help me get her in the truck."

"Forget it, man," countered Bobby. "It's no use.

That guy's a cop. That means there are other cops around. We've got to get out of here!"

"We can't just leave her here!" insisted Lalo.

"You're gonna fuck around and get us caught!" Bobby reached behind his back and pulled out a snub-nosed thirty-eight. "I say we go, Anyway, she's dead."

"The hell she is!"

Bobby raised the gun and fired twice into Miki's body. She jerked, then lay still.

"The hell she isn't."

Lalo stared up at Bobby, seeing Bobby's eyes wild and glassy. He had seen Bobby looking crazy before, but never quite like this. At the moment he looked capable of anything, including killing them all.

"Now let's get the rest of this stuff loaded and get the hell out of here," said Bobby quietly.

Lalo decided not to argue. Without further hesitation he picked up the crate of LAWS rockets Miki had been carrying. Seeing this, the others did the same. In less than a minute the last of the crates were loaded.

"Okay," breathed Bobby when they were finished, "let's get it on!"

Tex nodded toward Miki. "Hey, man, what about the body? We just going to leave it here? That don't seem like such a good idea. Maybe we ought to take it with us."

Tex started toward Miki, but Bobby waved him off. "Leave her. There's no way they can tie her to any of us, anyhow. Come on, let's make tracks."

Bobby and Lalo jumped into the truck cab, Bobby driving. The rest climbed in the back. The truck screeched away from the warehouse, one of its back doors banging open from the sudden acceleration. Bobby turned hard and shot off toward the main gate.

At the guardhouse Chamberlain had heard the gunshots, first one, then two closely spaced together. Now he heard the roar of an approaching engine and saw the headlights of the utility truck heading at him. He whipped out his revolver, leveling it at the oncoming vehicle.

62

Bobby saw the man with the gun ahead of him. He floored the accelerator.

"Stop!" screamed Chamberlain at the top of his lungs. "Stop! Stop!"

The truck kept coming. Chamberlain fired twice. The bullets smashed through the windshield, starring it, punching past Bobby into the metal bulkhead behind him. Bobby spun the wheel as Chamberlain fired again. The truck swerved, going into a skid. Bobby lost control and felt the tail end of the truck whipping around. The truck smashed into the guardhouse and crashed through it in an explosion of wood, metal, and glass. As this happened Chamberlain tried to jump out of the way, but the truck fishtailed toward him, and he was caught hard by the back fender. With a sickening crunch his body spun up through the air and landed fifteen feet away.

The truck crashed through the main gate, spun around out of control, and finally squealed to a halt. The engine stalled. Bobby twisted the ignition key and pumped the accelerator. The engine ground over, not catching.

"Come on, goddammit!" he swore furiously. "Come on, you mother bastard, come on!"

The engine sputtered, then roared to life. Bobby jammed the transmission into low. The truck screeched forward. At the corner he made a hard right and kept his foot down.

Eight blocks away, on Seventh Street, a black-and-white patrol car was rushing toward Pier Fifty in answer to Chamberlain's code three, officer needs assistance. Seconds later the utility truck roared through an intersection ahead. The two officers in the patrol car looked at each other in surprise.

"Jesus Christ!" swore one. "He must be doing sixty!"

"Let's go after them!" said his partner.

Roaring down Mariposa Street, Bobby heard the patrol car behind him before he saw it in the rear-view mirror. He floored the accelerator, but the geared-down utility truck was no match for the black-and-white, which caught up easily. As it tried to pass, Bobby swerved hard suddenly, crashing into the patrol car. The car dropped back, but continued to follow closely.

At the next corner Bobby pulled a hard right in an attempt to lose the pursuing police car, but it stayed right with him. The chase wound up and down the dark streets of China Basin, the utility truck neither gaining nor losing any distance between it and the black-and-white.

Suddenly the back door of the truck burst open, and Karl leaned out with a brand new AR-15 tucked under his arm. He took a bead on the patrol car and fired. The blast of bullets chewed across the front of the car, shattering the headlights, punching holes in the radiator. The officers, realizing what they were up against, dropped back quickly. Karl laughed and fired once more. This time the blast cut across the hood of the car, ripping the engine to pieces, shattering the windshield. The officer driving lost control. The patrol car suddenly swerved sharply up onto the curb, side-swiped a parked car, flipped over, and skidded down the street on its roof.

When it finally stopped the two officers clambered out of the overturned vehicle and scrambled away. Seconds later the punctured gas tank exploded. The patrol car erupted in a ball of bright flame which lit up the street for many blocks.

The two officers pulled their revolvers out and fired at the retreating truck. But their attempt was useless; the truck was by now too far away. Moments later they saw the taillights disappear around a corner.

"Son of a bitch!" shouted the officer who had been driving. He glared at the flaming remains of their car.

Then, since there was nothing else to do, the two men stood where they were, listening to the sound of approaching sirens.

Six

It was just after two a.m. that Harry Callahan's phone began to ring. He swore to himself, half asleep, and burrowed his head under the pillow, pulling it down over his ears to block out the irritating noise. It was useless. The phone kept ringing insistently, and finally Harry rolled over to answer it.

"Yeah? Who the hell is this?" His voice was tired and annoyed.

"Harry?"

"Who the hell else would it be?"

"This is Al Bressler." Harry snapped awake, forgetting his irritation. Bressler wasn't the sort to pull a man out of the sack at two in the morning just for the fun of it. "Frank DiGeorgio has just been stabbed. We're at the hospital now. You better get right over here."

Oh God, thought Harry with a sinking stomach, they got Frank. He sat up on the edge of the bed scrubbed his eyes with the heel of his hand ."How bad is it, Al?"

"It doesn't look good. Ralph Chamberlain was killed."

"What happened?"

"I'll tell you when you get here. And . . . Harry?"

"Yeah?"

"You better hurry."

Harry swallowed before answering. "Yeah. County Hospital?"

"Right."

"I'm on my way."

He slammed the phone down and dressed quickly. He was pulling into the big front parking lot of the San Francisco County Hospital on Potrero fifteen minutes later. The nurse at the information desk told him DiGeorgio was out of surgery and had been taken to the Intensive Care Unit in Ward Forty-three on the third floor. Harry took the elevator up, then wound his way down a maze of corridors, shuddering at the hospital smell of disinfectants and sickness.

He found Bressler leaning against the counter at the nurse's station, rubbing his eyes tiredly, waiting for him. There were two nurses on duty, one smoking a cigarette, the other reading a book. Harry ignored them, going directly to Bressler.

Bressler looked up, his eyes bloodshot. "Hello, Harry," he said thinly.

"How is he?" was Harry's first question.

"Irene is in there with him now. With a priest."

"That's supposed to be an answer?"

Bressler chewed on his lower lip, his big shoulders hunching in a helpless shrug. "He just had the last rites. What can I say? I'm sorry."

"Tell me about it, Al."

"We don't know all of it yet. Somebody broke into the warehouse down at Pier Fifty. They killed the old guard at the gate getting in. Frank and Ralph Chamberlain stumbled across what was happening in progress. They stabbed Frank and ran over Ralph with their truck on the way out. He was D.O.A." Bressler paused, running his fingers nervously through his hair. "On the way to the hospital Frank told us that the truck looked like a regular Gas Company job. I checked with the Marin Sheriff's Department—they had a Gas Company truck stolen over there last week. The two guys who were supposed to be driving it were found in a ravine, both dead. One of them was stabbed. Just like Frank. A waitress at a roadside diner in Mill Valley said she saw them pick up a girl who was hitchhiking. That could be something, or it could be nothing. We don't know yet, but we're looking into it. That's about all we've been able to trace out so far."

"What about the warehouse?" Harry was mulling it over in his head, already trying to connect the pieces together. "What did they steal?"

"We're still checking that part out. But it looks like guns and ammunition and explosives. That kind of stuff."

Harry sucked in a deep breath, letting it out slowly. "Revolutionaries?"

"Sounds like it could be."

"That's just what we need."

Bressler nodded toward the I.C.U. door. "He's been asking for you, Harry."

They went into the room. DiGeorgio was in a corner bed, an oxygen tube feeding into one nostril, an intravenous tube plugged into his arm, feeding him blood. Irene DiGeorgio was standing by the bed, wearing a bathrobe under her coat. Her face was pale and her eyes were watery. The priest was standing next to her.

"Hello, Harry," Irene said softly, as Harry put his hand on her shoulder, squeezing gently.

"Irene." There was nothing he could say.

The priest nodded, then went out into the hallway to wait.

"How is it?" asked Harry at last.

Irene clenched her teeth. It was obvious to Harry that she was close to her breaking point. Her voice quivered when she spoke. "He's in and out." Her hand sought Harry's, sliding over it, clutching it tightly.

In all the years Harry had known Irene DiGeorgio, he had never seen her cry, never seen her unhappy—until now. She had not liked being married to a cop, he knew, always afraid that one day something would happen. Now that it finally had, she was taking it very hard.

"Why did this have to happen?" she asked Harry, tears streaming down her cheeks. "Why?"

It was a question for which Harry had no answer.

He was a man without real religious convictions. Things happened or they didn't. The why of it was beyond his understanding.

Irene fought for control. "He told me once, 'Irene, if it's going to happen, it's going to happen. That's all there is to it. It's part of the job.' I guess I could just never understand that. He was the one going out there, but I was the one staying home, waiting. I asked him more than once to get a desk job, but he didn't want one. He thought it would be boring. He said that desk cops just took up space. He liked being out on the streets, where the action is, where he thought he was doing some good." She fumbled in the pocket of her coat, bringing out a pack of cigarettes. "I think I'll go out in the hall and smoke a cigarette." She gave Harry's hand a final squeeze, then went out quietly.

Harry moved closer to the side of the bed. DiGeorgio's eyes flickered open and focused on him.

"Hello, Harry." His voice was hardly a whisper. "Irene been giving you a hard time?"

Harry forced a smile. "A little."

"Talk back to her. Like I do."

"Are you kidding?" asked Harry. "She can whip you and me both, and you know it."

"Yeah . . . she's a tough broad."

"Tough as they come."

DiGeorgio winced, unable to conceal his pain. "Hey, Harry, look after her, huh?"

"You know that."

"You shoulda come over to dinner last night. That friend of Irene's showed up. A real looker. You would've liked her."

"Maybe next time I'll accept," offered Harry. "Besides, it's been a while since I had a real sit-down dinner."

"Careful or you'll end up a fat slob like me."

"No way." Harry leaned closer. "Frank—what happened?"

It took DiGeorgio a few moments before he could speak again. "I blew it, Harry. I had them dead. It was so damned stupid." He broke off, fighting a spasm of pain.

"Take it easy," said Harry.

Bressler came forward. "Frank? You said you wanted to tell something to Harry. You remember?"

DiGeorgio bobbed his head slightly. "Yeah, yeah. Harry, listen. I've seen him before. The punk who cut me. I only caught his face for a second. When he put the knife in. But I recognized him."

"From where?"

"That's just it. I can't make him. There's a face, but I can't put a name with it."

Harry and Bressler exchanged a glance. "Try to remember, Frank," said Harry. "Who is he?"

DiGeorgio was trying. "There was a homicide. You remember, Harry? A young black hooker up in the Fillmore District. I think it was maybe 'seventy-one. Summer."

Harry frowned, digging back for the memory. He recalled it vaguely. "What about her?"

"There was this guy. One of the pimps we questioned in connection with it. We liked him for it. We liked him a lot. But we just couldn't make it stick, he was too slippery. Remember? The D.A. wouldn't prosecute because we just didn't have enough hard evidence."

"As I recall we liked everybody north of Market for it," Harry said. "We questioned a lot of guys."

"Yeah, I know," whispered DiGeorgio. He was having trouble getting the words out. Harry leaned closer to hear. "He had one of those cutsie-pie little-boy names. If I could just make it out. Charley-something, maybe. Or Bobby." He grimaced. "Hell, I just don't remember. It was too long ago, but it was the guy. Harry. It was him."

"I can get Records to work on it," said Bressler. "They'll have your notes in the files. If you talked to the guy, we'll have the name."

DiGeorgio wheezed. "I'll bet you ten-to-one they don't get the guy."

"Sure they will. If I have to, I'll nail him myself. He's on borrowed time."

69

"Don't, Harry," advised DiGeorgio. "Don't take it personal. Don't let it get you like that. It's not worth it. Leave it to the department." There was another spasm of pain, stronger than the last one.

"You better rest," suggested Harry.

"You gotta go just yet?"

"Not if you don't want me to."

"I've been laying here, thinking back to the old days. Remember, right after you got married. We all of us had some times, huh? Remember that time we went up to Bodega Bay for the weekend? That was a lot of fun. Louise sure was one hell of a nice girl. Too good for you, I always said. I really miss her, Harry, I miss her a lot."

"Yeah."

DiGeorgio made a face as he saw Harry's expression. "I'm sorry, Harry. I wasn't thinking. Sometimes I got no sense. Hell, even dying I'm a dumb bastard."

"What dying?"

"Don't try to con a fat guinea. I know I ain't going to make it this time. That's okay, I don't mind. It's the breaks. Nobody lives forever, right? I'm surprised I made it this far. It's just Irene I'm worried about. Go over and see her sometime, will you?"

"I won't have to," Harry insisted. "You'll be out of here in a week, stuffing your fat face. Maybe you ought to think about taking that desk job, though."

"Bullshit," hissed DiGeorgio. "You may shoot good, Harry, but you don't lie worth beans." He shuddered, feeling another spasm. It was deeper this time, and longer. When he opened his eyes, they were filled with urgency. "Harry? I think you better get Irene . . ."

Harry reached out, taking DiGeorgio's hand for a moment, squeezing it. Then he went out into the corridor.

"Irene?" Harry called. "He wants you."

She nodded dully, dropping the stub of her cigarette on the floor, stepping on it. She paused to wipe her eyes dry with the back of her hand, then hurried into the room.

Harry walked over to Bressler, who was just hanging up the phone.

"You talk to Records?"

"Not yet. That was McKay again. We just got a tape from those bastards. It was found inside a phone booth across the street from the Hall of Justice."

Harry rubbed his fingers across his unshaven chin. "What does it say?"

"Don't know yet. Forensic's got it right now— they're almost done. I'm going over to McKay's office to hear it. When you get a chance, I'll meet you there."

"Right."

The door to DiGeorgio's room suddenly burst open. It was Irene, her face white, her eyes streaming with tears. "Nurse—please hurry!" she cried urgently.

One nurse jumped to her feet and ran into the room, followed by the priest. The other nurse picked up the phone and dialed two digits.

"Intensive care, emergency," she said into the receiver. "Code blue. Repeat: code blue." Then she hung up and hurried into the room also.

Bressler crossed himself. His voice was a whisper: "In the name of the Father and the Son and the Holy Ghost, Amen."

Two hours later Harry was sitting in Bressler's office, listening to a portable cassette tape recorder. It was four thirty-five in the morning.

The voice on the tape was a man's: young, cold, self-assured. "To the San Francisco Pig Department," the voice was saying. "Too long have the people of this nation been oppressed by the fascist government. This nation is a ripe boil about to be squeezed. We dedicate ourselves to the fight for freedom. We want one million dollars, for the cause of the people, or we will start blowing things up. We have the means and we have the will. The robbery of the warehouse at Pier Fifty is just a beginning. Unless you give us what we demand, more people will die. Power to the people! Power to the revolution! The People's Revolutionary Strike Force."

Bressler snapped off the tape. He picked up a cup of coffee and sipped it.

Harry sank back in his chair, putting his feet up on the edge of Bressler's desk. "What about the name? The People's Revolutionary Strike Force. Are they on the list of known militant groups?"

Bressler picked up a Xeroxed list and handed it over to Harry. "Nothing on them here."

Harry scanned the list. "You think it's a legitimate group, or just a rip-off attempt?"

"Who knows?" shrugged Bressler helplessly. "If you really want to get support in this nuthouse town, all you have to do is call yourself the People's Revolutionary Something-or-other. Christ, if you changed it to the People's Revolutionary Pneumonia, the Berkeley *Barb* would come out against penicillin tomorrow as a tool of the corporate fascist state. Sometimes I think they ought to throw a net over the whole Bay area and send them all off to Napa for the duration. It's getting so I don't know if there's anybody sane left any more. Including us."

"How about this warehouse robbery? Did you find out what they took yet?"

"Oh, yeah," Bressler muttered without enthusiasm. "Wait until you get a load of this. When I heard what they got, I just about peed in my pants." He picked up another sheet of paper and unfolded it. "Twelve AR-15 two-twenty-three-caliber automatic rifles. Seven thousand rounds of ammunition. Eighty pounds of dynamite —that's four crates of the stuff, twenty pounds to the crate. And get this one. LAWS rockets." He looked up from the list. "You know what they are?"

"Yeah," said Harry knowingly. "I've seen them demonstrated before. Nasty little bastards."

"That's what I hear."

"They can take out a whole goddamn building with one shot. With ten of them they could probably wipe out City Hall."

Bressler plopped the list on top of a stack of some other papers. "That's the lot. It was all waiting to be shipped to some army base in Korea. Somehow these

72

bastards found out about it. That's something for us to look into. How they found out it was all there to-night. Maybe one of them is a stevedore at the pier. Anyway, they must have some kind of connection. It could be a lead anyhow."

Harry leaned forward, glancing down the list of stolen items. "They've got enough stuff here to outfit an army. Hell, two armies even. Why are these bas-tards always better armed than we are? Someday I'm going to come up against one of these punks and he's going to shove a howitzer down my throat."

"Life is tough, Harry. Complain to the union."

Harry ignored the comment. "Any identification so far on the body of the girl?"

"Nope. We're still running the fingerprints through. Chew's working on that one right now. One of the lab boys says she had tracks on her arm. If we're lucky, maybe there's a drug arrest on her somewhere. We keep looking, we'll find a break somewhere. It's just a question of time."

"Time is one thing we don't have a hell of a lot of," Harry pointed out sourly.

Bressler leaned back and glanced out of his office window for a moment, watching the big red-and-blue neon sign on the side of the Union Seventy-six Building light up. "How's Irene?"

Harry's voice was emotionless. "Taking it bad. What do you expect?"

"Yeah, I guess. You see her home?"

"I drove her over to her sister's on Lombard." He pulled at the knot of his tie, loosening it, and un-buttoned his shirt collar. "She's going to arrange to have the body flown down to Pasadena."

"Pasadena?"

"That's where Frank was born. His folks are buried there."

"Oh." Bressler sat down, leaned on the desk, and buried his face in his hands. "God, I'm tired," he mumbled. "Didn't sleep last night either." When Bress-ler looked up, Harry saw that there were deep, dark circles under his eyes. "Used to be I could go a week

73

without sleep. I can't do it any more, though. I must be getting old."

"You are old," said Harry.

"Yeah?" Bressler sat up and shifted uncomfortably. "You're no spring chicken either, Callahan."

Harry shrugged. "I know it. A bunch of old men trying to run a police force. No wonder everything is so screwed up." He watched Bressler tiredly rub his eyes and fought back a yawn of his own. "Maybe you ought to try to sack out on one of the cots," he suggested. "You really look beat, Al. You're pushing yourself too hard."

"I'll be okay," insisted Bressler. "My daughter's graduation is tomorrow. I can sleep at that."

"Fran's graduating?"

Bressler flashed a proud smile. "She's giving a speech, too. She even got a scholarship to U. C. Berkeley for next year."

Harry laughed. "Going to be another student radical? Major in window-breaking and sit-ins."

Bressler was not amused. "She better not," he growled sharply. "I don't care if she is eighteen, I'll tan her ass good if she tries anything like that." His face softened. "She's going to take pre-med and be a doctor."

"That sounds real good," Harry said. He sometimes envied Bressler his children, his wife, his family life. It was something he did not have, nor, he realized somewhat sadly, would he ever have. Marriage and a family simply were not in the cards. He was too old and set in his ways. He had been a bachelor too long. If Louise had not died, things might have been different . . . but that was something he did not want to think about right now.

The two men subsided into silence. Harry stretched and yawned, unable to suppress the growing tiredness any longer, then suddenly had a thought.

"Hey, what about those records? They get anything on DiGeorgio's notes yet?"

Bressler snapped erect. "I forgot all about that. Hell, I called down there an hour and half ago. Wonder what's holding them up." He picked up the phone and dialed. "Hello? This is Lieutenant Bressler in homicide. What's happening on those records?" He paused. "A homicide in the Fillmore District. Inspectors Harry Callahan and Frank DiGeorgio. Nineteen seventy-one. I called you people over an hour ago. What's the stall?" Bressler listened, his face getting angry. "I'll be god-damned." He glanced at Harry. "They haven't even opened the files yet. Isn't that something?" Back into the phone he said, "What do you mean, you need a written request? Well, who has the keys, then?"

Harry got up and took the phone from Bressler. "This is Inspector Callahan," he barked into the receiver. "I'm going to be down there in ten minutes, and those files better be open by then. Because if they're not, I'm going to kick your ass from here to North Beach and back, you pencil-pushing son of a bitch! Do I make myself clear?" Harry listened a fraction of a second longer, then slammed down the receiver.

"Well?" Bressler asked.

Harry smiled. "He said he'd have them open."

Seven

By the time Bradford McKay walked into his office in the morning, Harry was already there waiting for him. He sat slumped in a corner of the room, a sheet of paper clutched in his hand, his face wearing a determined look. He made no effort to straighten up or stand as McKay entered.

Harry had spent the previous four hours going through all the notes and reports on file concerning the cases he and Frank DiGeorgio had worked on in nineteen seventy-one. It had been a formidable amount of material, comprising several stacks of thick file folders. More than once during the long hours he had felt himself starting to doze off, overcome with fatigue. He had forced himself to go on, drinking cup after cup of strong coffee, running on pure nervous energy. Half an hour ago he had at last found what he was looking for.

"Good morning, Callahan," McKay said briskly, looking fresh and rested in one of his expensive suits. He studied Harry's own wrinkled form. "You look as if you've been up all night."

"I have," admitted Harry. "I had some things to do."

"Callahan," said McKay, in the closest thing he had to a polite tone, "I just want to say right off that I'm sorry about Frank DiGeorgio and Ralph Chamberlain. I know DiGeorgio was a close personal friend of yours. He was also a damned good cop. They both were.

That was a terrible thing that happened last night."
McKay's voice was solemn, but it was about as sincere
as a wooden nickel as far as Harry was concerned. "I
talked to Mrs. DiGeorgio on the telephone this morning. She's a very brave woman. I think she's holding
up remarkably well under the circumstances."

You jerkwater bastard, thought Harry. I don't want
any of your phony piety. He wanted to tell McKay
that as far as he was concerned, Frank DiGeorgio dead
was a better man than McKay could ever be living.
He wanted to say a lot of things to McKay, but he
didn't. He had more important things to do than try
to let a little hot air out of the captain's stuffed shirt.
Besides, he couldn't afford to have McKay mad at him.
Not just yet, anyway, not to start off with. Maybe
later.

"I want to work on this," said Harry softly. His
voice was calm, but there was an unmistakable edge
to it. "There's no way you can stop me."

"You don't have to make threats," McKay countered.

"I'm not making threats. I'm just telling you, so
it won't be a rude surprise later. Because regardless
of anything or anyone, I'm going to nail the punk
who carved DiGeorgio, and I'm going to nail all his
lousy friends, whoever they are. I'll do it on my own
time if that's what it takes. I don't care about that.
But if you try to stop me or keep me out of it, then
you and I are going to tangle."

"I said that wasn't necessary," said McKay crisply.
His tone was as cold as ever, but he did not seem to
be angry. "You've been back on homicide since six
o'clock this morning. Didn't Bressler tell you that?"

Harry shook his head. "I haven't seen him since
before that. What made you change your mind?"

McKay sat down. "I'm not without feelings, Callahan, contrary to whatever you may think. I said I
realized that DiGeorgio was a good friend of yours.
I knew that you would want to work on the case. And
you have done good work in homicide in the past—
when you were able to control yourself. So. I'm willing
to give you another chance on this case. But let me

make a couple of things clear right at the beginning here. First of all, you will follow my orders, and you will act with restraint. I don't want any more incidents like that one we had a few days ago." McKay paused for a confirmation from Harry but got none. "Second," McKay went on, "I want you to treat this professionally. Despite your feelings, this is not a personal vendetta, it's another police assignment. Is that understood?"

"It's understood," replied Harry quietly.

"Then we both know where we stand."

"We do."

"Fine. Now what have you got so far?"

Harry sat up. "Before Frank died this morning, he said he recognized the guy who cut him. He didn't remember the name, but he remembered the case. He was sure the guy was a pimp involved in the killing of a Fillmore hooker a couple years back. So I've been down in records the past few hours checking through Frank's old notes."

McKay straightened a pile of papers on his desk. "Did you find anything useful?"

"This." Harry held out a list of names.

McKay checked the list without real interest. "Mandel, Boston, Cameron, Maxwell . . ." He glanced from the list to Harry. "Shall I tell you what my own instinct is on this one, Callahan? Black militants."

"Hookers keep coming up. We finally got an identification on that girl who was shot at the warehouse. Her name was Miki Waleska, known prostitute. Arrested twice in the last year."

"I don't know. This doesn't sound like the kind of thing a pimp would get involved in. What is a pimp going to do with all those guns and explosives?"

"Frank recognized the guy," Harry persisted.

"That doesn't necessarily mean anything. He was dying, Harry. He might not have seen who was really there. In situations like that, the memory sometimes plays tricks."

Harry was not convinced. "Frank DiGeorgio was a good cop. He knew what he saw. And his memory wasn't playing tricks on him. I talked to him in the hospital. I know. If Frank said he knew the guy who killed him, then you can bet your silk shorts he did."

"What we have here," insisted McKay, "is a well-organized group of militants—and they've got enough explosives to blow up half of San Francisco. Including dynamite and LAWS rockets."

"I've seen the sheet. You don't have to tell me."

"Every nut out there on the street is already gunning for the police. Every man on the force is little more than a moving target. Now we have this. As of right now, every available man is on the case, and you're the man in charge. Whatever you need to close it, Harry, let me know and you'll get it. The chief called down personally. He wants an arrest. And fast."

"Did he have any suggestions about who we should arrest? Or will just anybody do?"

McKay threw Harry a sour look. "Look into any and all militant and para-military groups for suspects, especially black militants." He looked up at the wall clock. "The army is going to give us a demonstration of LAWS rockets at the Presidio Firing Range in exactly thirty-five minutes. I'd like everybody who is involved in this case to be there. I want you all to see exactly what you're up against."

Harry stood up and started for the door. "Look, Captain, I've got a lot more important things to do right now than go out and watch the army play toy soldier and blow things up. Besides, I've already seen a LAWS fired."

"Just a minute, Callahan," barked McKay.

Harry stopped, looked back. "What is it?"

"Maybe you've seen a LAWS fired," smiled McKay, "but your partner hasn't."

"My what?"

"Your partner."

"What partner?" demanded Harry. "I don't have a partner any more, remember?"

"Wrong. You've just been assigned one. By me." McKay leaned over and pressed a button on his office intercom. "Miss Malave, will you please send in Inspector Moore?"

"Inspector *Moore*?" Harry had a sinking feeling in his stomach. There was something unpleasantly familiar about that name . . .

The door opened, and at that moment Harry knew why he'd had that sinking feeling. Standing in the doorway was Officer Moore, the policewoman he'd met a few days before in the Orals Board Room. The smart-ass broad who knew all the answers. So she had made the grade after all. And now she was an inspector in homicide. His partner.

"Oh, shit," muttered Harry to no one in particular.

McKay was in the process of introducing them. "Inspector Harry Callahan, this is Inspector Kathryn Moore."

"I prefer to be called Kate," Inspector Moore said. She gave Harry a rigid smile. "And Inspector Callahan and I have already met."

"Really?" beamed McKay. "Well, excellent." He was watching Harry's reaction carefully.

"Uh . . . Captain?" Harry's voice was hoarse with surprise. "If you don't mind, I'd prefer to work alone on this one. I don't really need a partner on this particular case. It would just slow me down and—"

"No one said you have a choice, Callahan," said McKay. "Either you work with Inspector Moore as your partner, or you go back to Personnel. Take your choice."

Harry suddenly realized that all of this was not just an accident. It was McKay's way of getting back at him. Dobbs had probably put pressure on the chief to get Harry out of his hair. McKay had been stuck. Kate Moore was McKay's way of punishing Harry for being a bad boy. You dirty bastard, thought Harry, you really did it this time, didn't you?

Harry wheeled around abruptly and walked out of McKay's office without another word. He was halfway down the hall before Kate Moore caught up with him.

"Inspector Callahan!"

Harry did not stop or even slow down. His long

81

strides forced Kate to take extra-long steps to keep up with him. She was literally running alongside.

"I want you to know," she began, "that I'm not any happier over this assignment than you are. Believe me, is wasn't my idea for us to be working together."

"Good for you," growled Harry without bothering to look at her.

"You don't think I'm up to this job, do you?"

"You really want to know what I think?"

"Yes."

"I think you're going to be a big pain in the ass."

They reached the end of the hall. Harry punched the button for the elevator as if it were a troublesome suspect. Kate stood panting for breath beside him.

"I think there's one thing we ought to get crystal clear," she said between breaths. "The fact that I am a woman is totally irrelevant from now on. I neither expect, nor will I stand for, any special consideration from you because of that fact. As far as I'm concerned, I want you to treat me simple as a fellow officer."

"Outstanding," Harry retorted. It was clear that he was not at all enthusiastic.

The elevator doors opened. Harry stepped inside. Kate was still standing in the hallway, glaring at him, skinning him alive with her eyes.

"Coming, Inspector?"

Kate stepped inside. "I think you have a negative attitude," she said.

The army firing range at the Presidio was a wide expanse of flat ground covered with short, sunburnt, brown grass. An old battered jeep, which had obviously not been running for many years, was parked at the far end of the field, apparently to be used as a target.

By the time Harry and Kate arrived, McKay and Bressler were already assembled with a group of other police department inspectors. Walter Martin, whom Harry knew to be the mayor's aide-de-camp, was standing nearby in low conversation with a big army sergeant.

"You're late," admonished McKay as Harry and Kate walked up.

"As usual," added Bressler.

"Don't blame me," Harry retorted crisply. "Inspector Moore here had to make a little stop at the powder room. That only took fifteen minutes."

Kate grinned sheepishly and looked at her feet.

"Don't be too hard on her, Harry," advised Bressler. "After all, it's her first day, remember?"

"I know," Harry replied grimly.

McKay nodded to the big army sergeant. "You can begin any time you're ready, Sergeant."

"Yes, sir." The sergeant picked up a LAWS rocket from a wooden crate at his feet. "Gentlemen—and ma'am—" he nodded briefly at Kate, who favored him with a pleasant smile—"this is an M-40 LAWS rocket. That is, a Light Anti-tank Weapons System rocket. The LAWS is, for all intents and purposes, a one-shot disposable, throw-away bazooka." He held up the fiberglass rocket launcher for them all to see, then handed it to Bressler to pass around. "You will note that it is much lighter and more compact than the conventional bazooka and is therefore substantially easier to carry. Also, unlike the conventional bazooka, which requires two men to operate it, one to load and one to fire, the LAWS can be used by a single soldier. It is a fiberglass tube, forty-five inches long, three inches in diameter, which is capable of firing a single projectile designed to penetrate armor plate to the thickness of three-quarters of an inch."

The sergeant waited while the LAWS was passed around the group. When finally it was handed back to him, he held it up in full view once more.

"Now if you've all had a good look at it, I'll demonstrate how it works. To fire the LAWS, you first pull this pin back here, removing the front and rear protective covers like so." The sergeant pulled the pin and the covers popped off. "Now you pull like this." He grabbed the fiberglass tube, one hand in the middle, the other on the back, and pulled. The tube telescoped open another eighteen inches. The front and rear sights popped up into place. "As you can see, when the rocket is fully extended, your front and rear sights automatically pop up into place. Then you take your safety off like this." He snapped a small lever. "Now the rocket is armed and ready to fire. Your trigger is right here." With one beefy finger he indicated a metal lump on the top of the tube. "Are there any questions so far?"

There were no questions. The sergeant looked at McKay. "Shall I proceed, Captain?"

McKay nodded. "Go ahead."

The sergeant moved away from the group, settled the LAWS on his right shoulder, and took aim at the target vehicle about fifty yards away.

Bressler turned to Harry while the group waited. "We just got word from pathology, by the way. They're doing an autopsy on that guard killed at Pier Fifty last night. It's scheduled for noon. You probably won't get anything useful, but it might be worthwhile to check it out."

"I'll do that," Harry said. He looked around to see that Kate had moved closer to the sergeant for a better look at the demonstration. She was standing directly behind the tail of the rocket launcher.

"Sweet Jesus," swore Harry. He hurried forward, reached out, and grabbed Kate by the collar, jerking her toward him.

"Hey!" she cried. "What are you doing—".

A split second later the sergeant fired the rocket. A bright billow of flame shot out of the launcher tail, shooting through the space Kate had occupied a moment before. The projectile, clearly visible as a round, flaming-red object about the size of a tennis ball, streaked out of the front end of the tube and struck the jeep. For a bare fraction of a second, nothing happened. Then, quite suddenly, the whole thing seemed to expand, then burst into flame and smoke. The noise of the explosion was deafening, echoing off the surrounding hills. A mushroom-shaped ball of fire, resembling a miniature atomic blast, rose from the burning jeep.

Kate just stood there, first staring at the flaming

remains of the target vehicle, then looking numbly at the spot where she had been standing. The tail flame of the LAWS rocket had blackened a six-foot area of ground and brush, which now smoldered darkly. It took little imagination to realize what would have happened to her had Harry not grabbed her when he did.

Captain McKay, who had missed the entire incident, now turned to the rest of the group. His expression was ominous. "Well, that concludes the demonstration. I hope you are all impressed with how dangerous a weapon like that is in the hands of the crazed revolutionaries we're dealing with in this case. Somehow we've got to find those people—and those weapons—before they find the opportunity to put them to use. That doesn't give us very much time, I'm afraid. We've got to work fast. Otherwise we're going to have a war on our hands, a war right smack in the middle of the streets of San Francisco. And we all know what that could mean. We're paid to protect this city from that kind of thing, so let's get to work."

Harry was already moving toward the car. He looked back at Kate, who stood where he had left her, still staring dazedly at the blackened spot of ground.

"Let's go—Inspector!" he called.

Kate snapped out of her reverie and trotted after him. As Harry opened the car door to get in, Kate swallowed and smiled at him with genuine warmth for the first time. "I want to thank you for what you did."

"Forget it," Harry snapped back at her gruffly. "It wouldn't do to let you get your ass burned to a crisp. Not on your first day on the job, anyway."

Eight

During the drive back to the Hall of Justice neither Harry nor Kate said anything. Harry glanced over at her every once in a while, but she now seemed to be ignoring him completely, keeping her eyes fixed on the passing streets.

Well, thought Harry with a trace of satisfaction, at least she doesn't talk much. If there was one thing Harry Callahan could not stand, it was a talkative partner. They would be yapping away, shooting the breeze, when something important happened. Besides, he did not like having to make conversation. Harry talked as little as possible, and often not at all. For one thing, there were just not very many topics of conversation that held any interest for him. Unlike other men, he did not talk about sports or women, the two major topics of male conversation. The only thing Harry knew and was interested in was his job. Police work. That was what he understood and did best. It didn't leave him much time for other things, but that did not bother him. It was what he liked to do. There really was nothing else.

Coming through the eastern end of Golden Gate Park, on Kennedy Drive, Harry caught their call number on the police radio. He turned up the volume.

"Inspectors seventy-one. Inspectors seventy-one."

Harry unhooked the microphone. "Inspectors seventy-one. Go ahead."

"Stolen gas company truck found in abandoned warehouse at Hunter's Point, corner of Kirkwood and Donahue, in abandoned warehouse. Over."

Harry thumbed down a button on the microphone. "Inspectors seventy-one responding. Out."

It was a big warehouse, dirty gray, with boarded-over windows and padlocked doors. One of the padlocks had been forced open, probably by a crowbar. Inside, the warehouse was almost completely empty, with the exception of some rusted machinery against one wall. Everything was thick with dust and dirt. The gas company truck had been parked in a far corner and abandoned. Whoever had been driving it, they had moved fast. The doors of the truck had been left standing open.

"There are two bullet holes in the windshield," Harry said to the lab technician on duty, Dave Yamamoto, a short Japanese whose drooping mustache gave him the appearance of a samurai pirate.

Yamamoto held up a small, clear plastic envelope. "I dug these out of the bulkhead inside. Offhand, I'd say they were from a three-fifty-seven." There were two deformed slugs in the envelope.

Harry took it from Yamamoto's hand and scrutinized the bullets closely. "Probably from Ralph Chamberlain's gun. There were two shots fired from it. He must have been able to get off a couple of quick ones before they ran him down." Harry handed the envelope back.

"Sorry about what happened to Frank," Yamamoto said. "Terrible thing."

"Yeah," replied Harry, his voice tightening. He did not want to talk about it any more. The rage it sent through him was a distraction he could not afford on the job. Talking about it was just a waste of time, anyhow. The only thing he could do for Frank Di-Georgio would be to nail the clowns. "How about fingerprints?" Harry asked, moving closer to the truck. "Find anything yet?"

Yamamoto shook his head. "It's been wiped clean.

Chances are we won't find a thing. We'll have a better look at it back at the lab. I'll let you know if we find anything. But I wouldn't hold my breath. These guys handled the job like professionals. They had to figure we were going to find this truck sooner or later, so they were probably very careful. I doubt if they left any clues behind."

Harry nodded. "How did you find the truck, anyway?"

"A watchman from the Naval Yard. He noticed that the padlock had been forced. He says he's sure it wasn't that way on Monday." Yamamoto pointed to a line of muddy tire tracks a dozen feet away. "Something interesting here, but I don't know what good it is. They had a second vehicle waiting here, probably to transfer the stolen goods into. Can't tell much from the tracks—they're too muddled. Even if we found the second vehicle I'd never be able to match them. But from the axle length and tire width, it must have been a van or a truck."

"It's something, but not much," agreed Harry. "Now all we have to do is go out and arrest every truck and van driver in San Francisco."

"I do my best," said Yamamoto.

Harry looked around. Kate was nowhere in sight. "Now where the hell has she gone to?" he muttered.

"You looking for your partner?"

Harry snarled. "Some partner. She spent the last nine years in Personnel and Records. She's going to be a big help."

Yamamoto laughed shortly. "Times are changing, Harry. Pretty soon we'll have a woman chief."

Harry looked horrified at the idea. "God," he said, "we should never have given them the vote."

Harry found Kate waiting for him back in the car. "I've been looking for you," he said as he got in. "Did you have to go to the powder room again?"

"I got the feeling you didn't want me around," Kate countered. "So I decided to stay out of your way."

Harry started the car. "Good idea," he told her.

"They'll be doing that guard's autopsy in about fifteen minutes in Pathology," she reminded.

"We'll make it." Harry back out of a cluster of official cars, shifted, and pulled out into the street.

"By the way," said Kate after a moment, "it's twelve-five in my gym shorts."

Harry blinked. "What?"

"My time for the hundred," she explained. "Remember? You seemed to think that it was important at the orals."

Harry looked at Kate, trying to figure if she was being nasty or just kidding him along. "You think I was picking on you, don't you?"

"To be brief and to the point, yes. Are you saying you weren't?"

Harry shrugged slightly. "I guess I was. It's nothing personal about you, though."

"What, then?"

"Well, I just don't think you have any real idea about what we do for a living in homicide."

"I'll find out, won't I?"

Harry eyed her narrowly. "I just hope you don't find out the hard way," he warned. "It can be really tough sometimes. There's nothing like finding a body with his head blown off by a shotgun blast to really ruin your day. And there's a lot worse than that. Things can get pretty grisly when it comes to corpses. It isn't like the movies. I can tell you stories that will turn your stomach. You'll see a lot of things you'll wish you hadn't."

"I've got a lot of stamina," Kate insisted. "I may surprise you. By the way, about your partner—"

Harry cut her off. "Yeah, I know, you're sorry. Everybody is sorry." His voice was brutal.

Kate was taken aback by his voice. "Excuse me."

Harry glanced over at her, realizing his tone had been too rough. "It's not you," he explained in a softer voice. "It's just that everybody who sees me now tells me how sorry they are about Frank. It's like a little speech they all deliver when I come around." His jaw tightened. "Besides, he wasn't the first partner I've lost."

Kate nodded carefully. "I know. I checked your records. Gerrard Fanducci, nineteen seventy, shot during an arrest of a big narcotics dealer. And Early Smith, nineteen seventy-four, blown up by a bomb that was put in his mailbox. But neither of them was your fault."

"Tell that to their widows," grunted Harry with a scowl. "They were my partners."

"Look," Kate said, "I don't want to get killed any more than you do. I realize I've got a lot to learn. That's why I'm here. But at least give me a chance. If I do something wrong, tell me. I can learn from my mistakes."

"Some mistakes you don't survive to learn from."

At this last remark Kate became silent again. She watched Harry from the corner of her eye, trying to figure him out, not being able to. He was a good policeman, she knew, in fact one of the very best. Among other things he had received four departmental commendations for bravery. But he was also a man who insisted on doing things his own way. Authority seemed to mean nothing to him, other than a hurdle in his path he must continually jump.

"By the way, Inspector," she asked suddenly, "how fast do you do the hundred?"

"Beats me," said Harry.

The Autopsy Room was in the basement of the Hall of Justice. It was all white tile and stainless steel, reeking of disinfectant. The naked body of the dead guard, Pop Siegel, partially draped with a white sheet, was lying on one of a long line of surgical tables. The surgeon, a mild-mannered little man with thick glasses, was giving a handful of intestines to his assistant as Harry and Kate walked in.

"Hi, Harry," beamed the surgeon. "Who's the pretty lady?"

Kate saw what the surgeon was holding and clutched Harry's arm.

"This is my new partner," Harry grunted, "Kate Moore."

"Nice to meet you, Kate." The surgeon held out a bloody gloved hand as a gesture of friendship. As Kate recoiled with horror, the surgeon grinned at his error. "Oh. Sorry about that."

The assistant took the intestines and dropped them into a large bottle filled with formaldehyde. The surgeon scribbled something on a paper label, peeled the backing off it, and stuck the label on the bottle.

"Well," he said to Harry a moment later, "I'm afraid you've missed some of it. We got back a little early from lunch, so we started early."

At the mention of the word "lunch," Kate swallowed sickly and closed her eyes.

"Couldn't help it," Harry said. "We got hung up on the firing range out at the Presidio. McKay gave us one of his 'Go out there and get 'em' speeches."

"Win one for the old gipper, eh?" The surgeon chuckled. "I always thought McKay would make a better football coach than a cop."

"You ought to tell him," suggested Harry hopefully. "Maybe he'll listen."

"Not me," said the surgeon quickly. "I like working here. Besides, in a couple of years I'll be ready for retirement." He turned to the guard's body. "Anyway, I've got it all on tape for you if you want to hear it. We just finished with the abdominal cavity."

"I don't need to hear about that. I'm just interested in the wound. Anything special about it?"

"Well . . . the entry wound was three quarters of an inch below the sternum, penetrated six inches up into the chest, severing the ascending arteries. With a wound like that, death usually occurs within a few seconds."

Harry saw Kate was looking greener every minute. "What kind of a knife did he use?"

"Long, heavy blade. Like this." The surgeon gestured with bloody fingers to indicate the length.

Harry considered. "Like a commando knife?"

"As a matter of fact, yes. That could well be. I'd

say it could be any one of those military killing knives, like maybe a Marine Corps Bowie or one of those Special Forces Randalls. You know the kind I mean."

"Any bruises on the face?"

The surgeon nodded. "There are definite indications that the killer clamped his left hand over the guard's mouth from behind."

"A real professional job."

"Textbook."

Harry frowned. "Sounds like the guy spent some time in Vietnam. That's how the Special Forces are taught to kill."

"We're going into the skull now, Harry, if you'd like to watch."

Kate tugged at Harry's sleeve and looked at him plaintively. "Do we . . . really have to?"

"It's part of our job," Harry replied curtly. "You said you were here to learn. Remember?" His voice was cold and unkind, which was exactly what he meant it to be.

The surgeon bent forward to study the guard's skull carefully. "No signs of exterior damage to the skull." He held out his hand. The assistant handed him a quarter-inch drill with a disc saw on the end. "Stand back," the surgeon advised. "We're going to lose some of this, I'm afraid. It gets rather messy."

Harry and Kate backed up, Kate putting her hand to her mouth. The surgeon turned on the drill and began cutting through the skull. Pieces of bone splintered off and whizzed through the air. Kate was again holding tightly onto Harry's arm.

"Subject brain shows no contracoup type injury nor blood clotting," said the surgeon, speaking above the whine of the saw into the tape recorder microphone suspended above. He finished cutting a hole in the top of the head and handed the drill back to his assistant. Both men bent over the body, peering into the opening in the skull.

"Jesus H. Christ, Harry!" gasped the surgeon suddenly. "Come here and take a look at this, God-damnedest think I ever saw!"

Harry pried Kate's hand off his arm and came forward. "What is it?"

The surgeon looked up and smiled, pointing into the hole. "It says *'Vote no on Proposition Fifteen'*!" The surgeon and his assistant broke into peals of laughter at their own joke. Harry looked at them both with grim resignation. Behind him, Kate made a sudden nauseated sound. Harry saw her run out of the room, hand clutched to her mouth.

"Gee," said the surgeon, sadly shaking his head, "no sense of humor."

Dressed in a well-tailored tan suit, carrying a snappy black leather briefcase, Henry Lee Caldwell looked like any other young and upcoming lawyer on his way into the Hall of Justice to see a client. Which was, of course, exactly the way he wanted to look.

Just inside the main door on Bryant Street, the foyer had been blocked off by a partition, leaving only one entrance into the rest of the building: a wooden arch that was connected to a metal detector. Two police security guards were on duty at the metal detector, checking incoming people one by one. Henry Lee stood in line, waiting patiently for his turn to be checked through.

"Take your keys and any metal objects out of your pockets, please," ordered one of the guards in a monotone each time a new person stepped up to the detector.

Henry Lee put his briefcase down on the table, then reached into his pocket, taking out his keys, a handful of change, and a metal comb, all of which he plopped down on top of the briefcase. The first guard waved him through.

Meanwhile the second guard opened the briefcase and went quickly through its contents: stacks of papers. He closed the briefcase and handed it back to Henry Lee, along with the rest of his things. Henry Lee pocketed the things and headed for the elevator. He pressed the down button.

When the elevator finally arrived, Henry Lee took

it to the basement level, stepped out, and headed down a long corridor. As he passed the police cafeteria, a roly-poly Chinese scoutmaster came out of the door and bumped into him.

"Sorry about that!" apologized the scoutmaster quickly.

"That's okay," replied Henry Lee.

The scoutmaster looked down the hall and spotted three young boys, about twelve, running in and out of open elevator doors. "Michael, Timothy, and Benjamin—if you're not in here before I count to ten . . ." The three boys ran back to the scoutmaster at full speed.

Henry Lee continued on down the hall, while the scoutmaster behind him scolded his charges loudly. Just past the cafeteria, Henry Lee went through a door marked MEN.

Inside the restroom, a man in a business suit was standing in front of the mirror over the sink, carefully combing his hair and patting it into place. Henry Lee paid the man no attention, heading straight for one of the toilet stalls. He closed the stall door behind him and latched it. Then he put his foot up on the toilet seat and rested the briefcase on his knee. Opening the briefcase, he took out the scattered papers inside, which he crumpled up and dropped into the john. Next he ran his fingers along the inside lining of the briefcase until he found a small fingerhold. He pulled on this until the entire lining wall came out. Concealed in the briefcase bottom were four bound-up sticks of dynamite connected to a battery and a timer. Henry Lee adjusted the timing device, setting it for one minute, and then snapped a toggle switch. A tiny red light flickered on. The sweep hand on the timer began to move backwards. He then replaced the fake lining wall, closed the briefcase, and locked it. He put his foot on the toilet handle and watched the crumpled papers gurgle down the drain.

Coming out of the toilet stall, Henry Lee saw the man in the business suit was still standing at the mirror, primping himself. Shit, thought Henry Lee, what is this guy, queer for himself?

Henry Lee walked over to the sink, put the briefcase down on the floor, and began washing his hands, taking his time. Finally the man in the suit left. When he was gone, Henry Lee waited a few moments to see if anyone else would come in. No one did, so he lifted the top off the trash can and put the briefcase inside, covering it with crumpled towels. Then he put the top back on the trash can, adjusted his tie in the mirror, and left.

Nine

Harry found Kate standing in the hallway just outside the Autopsy Room, bending over a metal trash can. She was not throwing up, but she did not look very well, either.

"You okay?" Harry asked, trying not to sound too concerned.

Kate whirled at him, her eyes bright with anger. "Yes, I'm okay!" she said furiously. "Not that it's any of your damned business!"

Harry was surprised at her fury. He suddenly understood that perhaps she was not as soft as he had first thought. Get her mad enough and she could probably give you one hell of a fight. That, at least, was something.

"Look, Inspector," he advised, "don't get mad at me just because you can't take it. I'm not the one who put in for a promotion I couldn't handle. You did that yourself. You wanted the job, and now you've got it. You don't like it? Well, that's tough. Nobody said you would!"

"All right!" shouted Kate. "I don't like it and I can't take it! Are you satisfied now! I'm just a silly, childish woman who throws up when she sees a little blood. Congratulations, Inspector Callahan, you've made me feel like two cents."

"That's not what I wanted—"

"Oh, yes, it is! That's exactly what you wanted!"

Harry jerked his thumb toward the door to the Autopsy Room. "Look, they were just joking around back there. You haven't seen anything yet. It doesn't get easier from here on in, it gets rougher. If you can't handle it, don't blame me. And don't go crying around, feeling sorry for yourself."

Kate sniffed defensively. "I'm not feeling sorry for myself."

"The hell you're not. You want to cry on somebody's shoulder, do it someplace else. I haven't got the time."

"I'm not crying," she said, pulling herself together. She wiped her eyes just to make sure.

Harry nodded. "Well, welcome to homicide, sweetheart," he said coldly.

At that moment there was an explosion. Harry and Kate were both rocked by the impact, Harry grabbing the wall for support, Kate grabbing Harry. Down the hall, past the cafeteria, Harry saw the door to the men's room blow open.

"My God," whispered Kate.

Harry did not bother to answer. He was already hurrying down the hall to the men's room. The door lay in the hallway, blown in half by the force of the explosion. The bathroom was a shambles. Mirrors were shattered, sinks were wrenched from the walls, the ceiling had a big dent in it. A geyser of water shot from a ruptured pipe.

A policeman appeared behind Harry. "What happened?" he asked above the noise.

"A bomb," said Harry. "You better get a janitor with a wrench down here to shut that water off right away."

The policeman nodded and ran off. Another officer, a detective, pushed past the crowd that was already forming. Harry recognized him as an inspector from the burglary division, Al Tinker.

"Was anybody in there when it went?" Tinker asked.

"I don't think so," said Harry.

Tinker stared at the shambles, shaking his head. "What a mess!"

Harry nodded. "Yeah. It's getting so you can't even go to the can in peace any more."

As Tinker checked the restroom, Harry went back into the hall. The roly-poly scoutmaster was trying to push his way into the bathroom.

"Where are you going?" demanded Harry.

"Two of my kids are missing," howled the scoutmaster.

"They're not in there," Harry said. "I think I saw them getting into an elevator a second ago."

The scoutmaster breathed a sigh and wiped his forehead with a sleeve. "Thank God," he whispered.

Where were you when it happened?" asked Harry suddenly.

The scoutmaster motioned down the hall. "In the doorway of the cafeteria. There was a big cloud of smoke, and the next thing I knew—"

Harry broke in quickly. "Did you see anybody go in there before the explosion?"

The scoutmaster shook his head. "No—wait a minute, yeah. Come to think of it, I did."

"What did he look like? It's important."

The scoutmaster thought.

"Well?" demanded Harry. "Tell me!"

"He was a big black guy, about six feet tall." He held up his hand to indicate the man's size.

"What was he wearing?"

"Um—a tan suit. And he was carrying a briefcase." The scoutmaster's eyebrows went up. "But he didn't have it when he came out!"

"A tan suit," Harry repeated. "Okay, thanks. Hey—you didn't see which way he went, did you?"

The scoutmaster hadn't.

"But I did."

Harry turned around to see Kate standing behind him. "What? When?"

"I was in the hall, barfing my brains out, remember? He was in a hurry. I thought it was kind of funny."

"Well," snapped Harry, "which way did he go?"

"Oh. Out the side door. To the left."

Harry took off at a run.

"Hey!" Kate called after him. "Wait for me!"

Moving down Bryant Street, Harry's eyes searched the passersby, checking their faces and clothes. Hippies, straights. Old people, young people. Men, women, children. Blacks, whites, Chicanos, Orientals. Talls and shorts. But not the man he was looking for.

And then Harry saw him, a tall black man in a tan suit, moving quickly through a crowd of people ahead, doing his best not to be seen.

"Inspector Callahan! Wait!" Behind him, Harry heard Kate's voice. "Wait for me!"

Goddammit, thought Harry, if she doesn't shut up, he'll hear her.

"Inspector Callahan!"

The black guy looked around and saw Harry moving toward him. He began to run.

Harry cursed internally and ran after him.

"Inspector Callahan! Wait for me!"

The black guy suddenly bumped into a pedestrian, knocking him down. There was a commotion, and Henry Lee Caldwell suddenly found himself blocked in by a curious crowd. Behind him he saw Harry running at him, closing in. With a feeling of panic, he shoved the people out of his way and bolted across the street.

"Hey—watch where you're going, man!"

Henry Lee ignored the shouts of protest, dodged around the front of an oncoming car which screeched to a halt within inches of him, and ran down a narrow alley.

Across the street Harry saw Henry Lee disappear down the alley. From his knowledge of the area, he remembered it was a through street that came out on Brannan, one block over. Harry ran across in front of the traffic at the intersection and went down Sixth Street at full speed, parallel to the alley. He tore around the corner onto Brannan just as Henry Lee appeared at the mouth of the alley, half a block down. Henry Lee saw Harry, spun around, and ran like hell up Brannan.

Harry looked after him. They galloped down the sidewalk, both running at full speed. At the next corner, Seventh, the intersection was jammed with cars backed up by a stalled truck ahead. Horns were honking loudly as Henry Lee skidded to a halt at the curb. Suddenly he jumped on the hood of the car in front of him, then leaped onto the roof.

"Hey, asshole!" the driver roared angrily. "Get off my goddamn car!"

Henry Lee ignored the driver and jumped onto the next car roof, and then the next, and so on, all the way across the street. When he reached the other side, he leaped down to the sidewalk and tore off down the street again.

Harry skidded up to the traffic jam, seeing what had happened. Without hesitation he leaped onto the hood of the nearest car and repeated Henry Lee's performance, accompanied by shouts and threats from drivers.

Past the jammed intersection Harry saw Henry Lee dodge into a doorway. Harry ran to the building, saw it was one of those off-Market fleabag hotels, and hurried inside. The lobby was dirty and smelled of dust and body odor. Harry glanced around, but saw no one except a mousy, frightened clerk cowering behind the desk.

"A guy just ran in here!" shouted Harry. "Where did he go?"

The clerk shook his head. "I don't want to get involved!" he moaned.

Harry had neither the time nor the patience to coax an answer. He reached across the counter, grabbed the clerk by the front of his shirt, and literally dragged him over the top. Picking him up off the ground, Harry slammed him up against the wall. The clerk grunted in pain.

"I said where did he go?" roared Harry.

The clerk looked as if he was going to have a coronary attack any second. He jerked one finger out. "The back alley!" he cried in absolute terror. "He went out the back alley!"

Harry let go of the clerk's shirt, dropping him like an old rag. The clerk fell on the floor in a heap. Without further speech or concern, Harry whirled and ran down the hallway the man had pointed to. He saw a door at the back just swinging shut. He kicked it open to see Henry Lee disappear around the corner of an alley. Harry thundered after him.

Henry Lee skidded around the alley corner and ran for all he was worth. Ahead, a wooden fence blocked his way. Reaching it, he leaped, caught hold of the top, dragged himself up kicking, and swung over the top. He dropped to the ground on the other side and ran on.

Seconds behind him Harry reached the fence and, without even bothering to try to leap it, simply crashed through it like a steam locomotive.

A shot exploded past Harry's head. He ducked and pulled up against the wall. Henry Lee was crouched in a doorway, had pulled a revolver, and was firing at him. Harry reached into his tweed coat and tugged out his big Magnum.

When Henry Lee saw the big long-barreled Magnum forty-four, his stomach sank. He pointed his own revolver at the locked door behind him and fired at the latch. The latch and knob exploded in a spray of metal. He kicked the door open and ran down a dark hall inside.

Harry squeezed the trigger of the huge Magnum a fraction of a second after Henry Lee disappeared inside, his bullet chewing away a piece of the doorframe at the spot where Henry Lee's head had been. Harry cursed and ran after him, through the open door, down the dark hallway.

Ahead and above him Harry heard the pounding of footsteps. At the end of the hall he found a stairwell leading up. Taking the stairs three at a time, Harry pounded up after him.

It was a long way to the roof—six flights plus the basement—and Henry Lee was nearly exhausted by the time he stumbled out onto the roof. He leaned against the doorframe, breathing like an asthmatic.

Behind him he could hear the pounding of Harry's footsteps on the stairs. Christ almighty, thought Henry Lee, doesn't the bastard give up?

He looked around desperately for someplace, anyplace, to hide. But there was no cover in sight, only an open, bare roof decorated with an occasional TV antenna twisted at a funny angle. Beyond the edge of the roof he could see another roof, at about the same level. There was a gap between them, but maybe, just maybe, he could jump it. There was no time to consider the situation, and there were no alternatives, so without further hesitation, Henry Lee began running again.

He galloped across the roof, long-striding, hurdling obstacles like a world champion steeplechaser.

Harry lunged out onto the roof, gasping for air. Thirty feet away he saw Henry Lee running.

"Police officer!" Harry wheezed. "Halt!" It was barely more than a whisper. He raised the Magnum to take aim, but his hand was so unsteady he could not fire.

Nearing the gap between the two buildings, Henry Lee suddenly realized that the distance he had to jump was much wider than he had thought. It had to be eighteen feet! He couldn't make it—there was no way! And it was a six-story drop . . .

But it was too late to stop. With as much strength as he could muster, he jumped, streaking across the gap. There was a two-foot brick ledge around the roof of the second building. Henry Lee stretched for it, landing with a painful grunt, his legs hanging off into space. He pulled himself up and scrambled onto the roof. The palms of his hands were scraped and bleeding. In another second he was on his feet, running like a zombie, too tired and exhausted to see where he was going. He crashed full tilt into a television antenna, falling, tearing it down with him. Somehow he managed to get up and stagger on.

On the other roof, Harry, having recovered some of his breath, was running again. He reached the gap between the two buildings, screwed up his face, and leaped off. He came down hard on the opposite roof, landing on his hands and knees, skidding across the gravel and tar paper. As he got up, he looked at the knees of his pants and the sleeves of his coat, both torn to shreds. Another goddamn suit down the drain. That made two this week. At this rate, his wardrobe would be wiped out in another month.

Harry looked up to see Henry Lee stumble through a line of hanging laundry, carrying off a brassiere and a pair of panties with him. Harry raised the Magnum and took aim.

"Freeze, you bastard!" Harry yelled.

Henry Lee continued to run. Harry waited a second longer, then fired. The big Magnum bucked in his hand, the boom echoing across the rooftop. The bullet chewed up a piece of roof a couple of feet in front of Henry Lee. The black man skidded to a halt, then dodged to the right. Harry aimed and fired again. The bullet slammed past Henry Lee's ear. He let out a yell of consternation, lost his footing, and slipped down a slanted roof. Harry saw the black man disappear from view. Scrambling for a foothold, Henry Lee slid down the slant and crashed through a dirty skylight with a scream.

He landed in a heap on something soft.

"What the hell is going on?" yelled a voice.

Henry Lee rolled over and saw the something soft he had landed on was a girl, naked as a jaybird.

"Get your fucking foot out of my face!" the girl screamed at him.

Henry Lee did as he was told. The girl kicked at him, landing a good one in his stomach. With a grunt Henry Lee went back and down, landing hard on his butt in the corner. He blinked, blinded momentarily by bright lights. Seven or eight people were standing around in a semicircle behind a sixteen-millimeter movie camera mounted on a tripod. Three of them, besides the girl Henry Lee had fallen on, were naked—two more women and one man. They were all staring at the black man numbly.

"Will you kindly explain what you mean by this?"

demanded the man nearest the camera. He spoke with a slight lisp and sounded gay.

"Goddamn creep!" shouted the girl at Henry Lee. "You nearly broke my neck!"

Henry Lee stared at them all wildly, not sure if they were real or a dream. He waved the gun at them. "Out of my fucking way!" he cried.

The girl screamed. "He's got a gun! Look out!"

"Oh, my God!" moaned the man with the lisp.

Henry Lee staggered to his feet and ran, pushing the group of people out of his way, knocking over the camera as he went. He threw open the door and ran down a dark hallway.

"Crazy maniac!" shouted the man with the lisp, bending over his fallen camera.

The girl screamed again. "Look. Another one!"

The rest of the group turned in time to see Harry drop through the smashed skylight, clutching his Magnum.

"He's got a gun, too!" howled the girl hysterically.

The lisping man clutched the camera and held it dearly to his chest. "Will you please tell me what is going on here?" he insisted. Anger made his lisp worse.

"I'm a police officer," growled Harry.

"Or, my God!" moaned the man. "It's a bust!" He rolled his eyes like Betty Boop.

Harry looked at the naked man, who was staring at him with wide, frightened eyes. "Why don't you go put some pants on?" Harry advised. Without bothering to wait for an answer he pushed past the man and ran through the door.

At the end of the hall Harry saw an elevator door just closing, his quarry inside. Harry halted, raised his forty-four, and fired twice. The bullets punched through the door, past Henry Lee's head, through the elevator wall behind him, and ricocheted off the concrete wall of the elevator shaft.

Harry ran to the elevator door and hooked his fingers in the slot where the doors joined, trying to pry them open. It was impossible. He looked up at the indicator lights over the door. The elevator was going down: six . . . five . . . four. . . .

Looking around, Harry saw an open doorway leading to a stairwell. He ran for it, bursting down the stairs, taking four or five steps at a time.

In the elevator Henry Lee was watching the floor lights flash past, hoping, praying that the cop, the crazy fucking cop, would not be able to catch him. Three . . . two . . . one.

The doors slid open. Two old women were waiting to get inside.

"Look out, bitch!" snarled Henry Lee, shoving the women aside like garbage. He ran out into the apartment building lobby. The cop was not in sight. Then he saw the stairwell and heard Harry's pounding footsteps. No, God! He was still coming!

The moment Harry came out of the stairwell door, Henry Lee fired. The bullet slammed past Harry, missing narrowly. Harry ducked back into the stairwell. Henry Lee fired off another quick round for good measure. Then he ran through the side doorway.

Hearing the retreating footsteps, Harry came out of the safety of the stairwell as Henry Lee disappeared out the door. Harry threw the door open to find himself in another back alley. He tore down the alley as fast as his legs would carry him, which really wasn't all that fast considering how much he had been through. He saw the black man kick open a gate of some kind and then disappear from sight.

Through the gate Harry found himself in some kind of back yard behind a red brick building. The black man was not in sight—but there was only one place he could have gone, and that was through the back door of the brick building. The rest of the yard was a dead end, and the surrounding walls were too high to climb.

Harry tried the door and found it locked. Bracing himself, he kicked it open. Ahead he saw Henry Lee charging down a hallway.

"Stop!" Harry yelled.

Henry Lee whirled, snapping up his revolver. He

106

pulled the trigger, but nothing happened. The chamber was empty. He threw the gun at Harry. It bounced harmlessly off the wall. Harry ran and jumped, tackling Henry Lee as he ran. They skidded through the doorway at the end of the hall, across an expanse of red carpet. Henry Lee struggled to get away, but Harry finally managed to pin him and jammed the Magnum in his face.

"All right, speedy," Harry wheezed, "unless you want a bullet sandwich, stop right now!"

Realizing further struggle was useless, Henry Lee stopped fighting. Harry rolled him over, dragged his hands behind his back, and cuffed him.

"Who are you?" an angry voice boomed across the room at Harry. "What is the meaning of this?"

Harry looked up, seeing a priest hurrying toward him. Surprised, Harry for the first time looked around, seeing where he was: in the sanctuary of a small Catholic church.

"Christ!" groaned Harry, pulling Henry Lee to his feet. "Where are we?"

"I'm Father John Voss, and you happen to be in my church—St. Ambrose," said the priest. "Tell me what you are doing here!" He was a young man, about thirty, with curly black hair and a bushy mustache.

"I'm a police officer," explained Harry between breaths. "I'm arresting this man in connection with a bombing at the Hall of Justice."

"It's a lie, father!" bleated Henry Lee. "I didn't do a damned thing! He's just rousting me!" He tried to pull away, but Harry grabbed him by the arm. "Man, you're breaking my arm!" Again he struggled to pull away.

"I want to see your credentials," demanded the priest.

Harry had his hands full, trying to keep his prisoner from pulling away.

"I said I want to see some identification," the priest insisted.

"Father, this guy's going to run if I let go of him!"

Harry explained. Henry Lee elbowed him sharply in the stomach.

The priest persisted. "Let me see those credentials right now!"

"Okay," said Harry, "if you insist." Raising the Magnum, Harry spun Henry Lee around on his heels, smashing the butt of the gun across the black man's skull. Henry Lee dropped like a pole-axed steer.

Harry reached into his pocket, withdrawing his star.

"What's your name?" asked the priest.

"Callahan. Inspector Harry Callahan."

"Well, Callahan, you're a disgrace to this city."

At this moment, the front doors of the church burst open, and Kate, disheveled and exhausted, lurched inside, gun drawn. "All right!" she gasped. "Don't anybody move!"

Harry glared at her, shaking his head slowly. "Outstanding," he muttered disgustedly.

Ten

As Harry walked into homicide, Ken Chew came out of the interrogation room.

"How's it going?" Harry wanted to know.

"We found a box of dynamite in his closet," said Chew. "Also two shotguns and an AR-15. The serial number on the AR-15 matches one of the stolen weapons."

"They getting anything out of him?"

Chew shrugged. "Like a clam. He doesn't know what we're talking about; he never heard of any dynamite. You know, the usual stuff. Personally, I think the guy's definitely antisocial."

Harry went into the interrogation room. The black man he had arrested, Henry Lee Caldwell, was being questioned by Rich Anderson and another detective, Joe Fuhrig, a big man with bags under his eyes. Harry nodded to both of them and sat down to listen.

"Where did you get the dynamite?" Anderson asked.

"What dynamite?" replied Henry Lee. "I keep telling you guys I don't know anything about any dynamite!"

"You're lying," said Fuhrig flatly. "We know you're lying, so why don't you just cut it?"

"I'm not lying," Henry Lee insisted. "You guys are just rousting me." His face was glistening with perspiration. "Why don't you just leave me alone, man?"

"We want to know a few things first," said Fuhrig. "Like that robbery at Pier Fifty. Who else was in on it with you? We know you didn't pull it alone. What are their names?"

Henry Lee gave a short, nervous laugh. "Man, I don't know what the hell you dudes are talking about. I didn't have nothing to do with that robbery, you know?"

"Three people were killed in that robbery, buddy," Anderson said. "A guard and two cops. And each one of them counts as murder one. Killing cops means you can die in this state—we've got the death penalty again, remember?"

Henry Lee swallowed thickly and looked away.

"You want to take that rap all on yourself?" Fuhrig asked. "That's a long, hard fall. Now, if you cooperate and give us the other names, we can talk to the D.A. and the judge—"

"Fuck you!" sneered Henry Lee. "You pigs don't scare me! You think you're all so goddamn smart, don't you? Well, you're not. Before this thing is over, I'll be free as a bird, man. My friends aren't going to leave me in here." He laughed harshly. "You want to charge me with murder, you go right ahead. You do whatever you want. I could care less."

Harry slowly stood up. "You've got all the answers, haven't you—punk?"

"Fuck off!" Henry Lee said defiantly. But he eyed Harry's huge frame uneasily.

"You've got a regular college vocabulary, don't you?"

Harry pulled his chair over next to Henry Lee's, very close, and sat down, practically breathing into the black man's face. "Let me tell you something, asshole," Harry began. His voice was deceptively soft. "Those two cops you killed were guys I knew. That's one. And one of them was a real close friend from a long, long time. That's two." He smiled and put his arm around Henry Lee's shoulder. "Now the thing is, if you don't tell us who the guys were that helped you, I'm personally going to stomp your ass until the shit squeezes out. You hear what I'm saying?"

"You can't do anything to me," said Henry Lee

110

nervously. "I've got rights." But it was plain to see that he was worried.

"Rights?" whispered Harry. "I never heard of the word. It doesn't mean a thing to me. I'll tell you something else. Even if you get off, there's still me. I don't care where you are, I'll track you down and find you. And when I do, I'll ram my gun down your throat and blow your brains out from the inside. When I'm done, they'll have to bury what's left of you in a rubber bag."

"Leave me alone!" bleated Henry Lee, trying to back away. "You don't scare me."

Harry blocked his retreat. "Now I want you to cooperate. Tell me where you got the dynamite."

"How should I know where that dynamite came from? Maybe the Easter Bunny brought it."

Harry showed his teeth. "That's real funny. I see you've got a sense of humor." Suddenly Harry hooked his foot under Henry Lee's chair and yanked it out. The chair went down. At the same time Harry grabbed him by the neck and slammed him up against the wall.

"Where did you get the dynamite?" Harry roared.

"I don't know any dynamite!"

Harry banged Henry Lee's head off the wall hard. There was a dent in the wall where a piece of plaster chipped off.

"The dynamite, asshole!"

"Get him off me!"

Harry began banging Henry Lee's head against the wall rhythmically. Anderson and Fuhrig jumped to their feet, trying to drag Harry back.

"Come on, Harry! You'll kill him!"

"Who are they?" shouted Harry. Bang, bang! "Who are they?" Bang, bang!

Suddenly the door burst open, slamming against the wall.

"What the hell is going on here?" Lieutenant Bressler demanded.

Harry let go of Henry Lee's head. He shrugged at Bressler. "Nothing. Our suspect just fell down and hurt himself." Harry smiled benignly at Henry Lee. "You should be more careful, friend. You could really get hurt."

Henry Lee looked fearfully at Harry, deciding he'd better not say anything.

Bressler obviously did not believe a word of it. "Harry, I want to see you in my office right now."

With a parting look of menace at Henry Lee, Harry went out and into Bressler's office.

"Goddammit, Harry," growled Bressler as he closed the door. "Was that necessary?"

"Maybe not," admitted Harry, "but it sure as hell made me feel better."

Bressler shook his head. "You just never learn, do you? If McKay heard about that little incident, he'd have you off homicide and you'd spend the rest of your life directing traffic on the Golden Gate Bridge."

Harry straightened his tie and smoothed down the lapels of his coat. "I was just trying to save us some time."

Bressler went around his desk, opened a file cover, and picked out a yellow sheet of paper. "We've got a make on your man. His name is Henry Lee Caldwell. Long record of arrests. Couple of convictions. Did time at Soledad. He's a member of a local black militant group called *Uhuru*."

Harry frowned. "*Uhuru*?"

"It's a Swahili word. Means *freedom*."

"Yeah, I've heard of them."

Bressler handed Harry the yellow sheet. "They've got their headquarters in a rundown old barber shop down in the Fillmore District, on Sutter. The leader is a guy called Big Ed Mohamid."

Harry rubbed his chain. "Sure. But I can't see them getting involved in anything like this. They sure don't like cops, but they've never been involved in violence."

"There's a first time for everything," said Bressler. "Anyway, McKay wants you to go down there and check it out. He's convinced that the robbery was set up by black militants. He's trying to get a search warrant for the *Uhuru* headquarters now. He figures they've got the guns and dynamite stashed there. I want you and Inspector Moore to get down there first."

Harry glanced around. "Speaking of my empty-headed partner, where the hell is she, anyhow? Every time I turn around, she's gone again."

"I talked to her about ten minutes ago. I think she went to the ladies' room."

Harry grunted. "Again? What the hell does she do? Live on the can?"

"Hey, Harry?" Bressler's voice was plaintive. "I know you're not thrilled with having her for a partner—"

"That's an understatement."

"But you hate everybody anyhow. Anyway, what I'm trying to say is, why don't you take it a little easy on her? At least give her a chance."

Harry was unmoved. "If she wants to play lumberjack, she's supposed to climb trees just like the rest of the boys. Isn't that the way it goes?"

"Yeah. Sure. I guess so."

"All right, then." Harry started for the door.

"You sure are one tough, dirty bastard," Bressler said as Harry opened the door.

Harry looked back, grinning from ear to ear. "Yeah," he said, "I know."

The old barber shop that now served as the headquarters for *Uhuru* was flanked by deserted boarded-up buildings on Sutter, just around the corner from Fillmore. Harry parked half a block away, just so he wouldn't spook anybody. In areas like the Fillmore District, people could tell cops a mile away, and Harry had decided he wanted to show up unannounced.

Kate was silent as they got out of the car, studying the dirty, abandoned buildings, the garbage on the sidewalks, the winos huddled in empty doorways with bottles in brown paper bags.

"I guess you don't see many places like this working in Personnel," said Harry with more than a touch of sarcasm.

"I grew up in Hunter's Point," said Kate. "On

Ingalls Street. It looks a lot like this. I used to play in a vacant lot and in the streets, too."

Harry was surprised, but he tried not to let it show. "That's supposed to impress me?" he retorted gruffly.

"No," replied Kate. "I don't think that's possible."

"You're right," Harry agreed. "It isn't."

The front of *Uhuru* headquarters was painted black. The name *Uhuru* was painted across the door in red, white, and green. A black nationalist flag, in the same three colors, had been painted in the blacked-out plate-glass windows on either side of the door. A couple of young black men in colorful dashikis were leaning in the doorway. As they saw Harry and Kate approach, they suddenly ducked inside.

"Looks like we're going to be announced," Harry noticed. "Welcome to the Fillmore chapter of the VFW."

Kate cocked an eyebrow. "VFW? What's that?"

"Very Few Whites," explained Harry. "I don't suppose it would do any good to suggest that you wait outside, Inspector Moore?"

"Don't worry about it, Inspector Callahan."

"I won't. But just remember, don't look to me for help."

"I'll keep that in mind."

The inside of the *Uhuru* building was old and in disrepair. The walls were decorated with black militant posters and large photographs of people like Huey Newton, Malcolm X, Bobby Seale, and Marcus Garvey. On the back wall was a painted outline of Africa, with South Africa and Rhodesia painted white. Below this were the words *Free South Africa and Rhodesia now! Black Africa for Black People!* Several young black men, most with big, fuzzy, combed-out naturals and thick beards, were shooting pool. Several more were playing cards nearby. There was a low hum of conversation which stopped abruptly as Harry and Kate entered. The blacks sat looking at the two white detectives, the hostility hanging thickly in the air.

"Well, well, well," said one of the blacks, the

114

smallest, as he got up and strutted toward Harry and Kate, "if it ain't Mighty Whitey and friend."

"White boys ain't allowed in here," said another, a big man with heavy sideburns.

"Yeah, baby," agreed the little one, "you know, niggers only."

"I'm looking for Ed Mohamid," Harry said evenly.

"Sorry, honky. The chick can stay, but you got to go."

"You know how it is, man. We're trying to keep up the standards."

Harry did not move. "You better watch out, or you're going to make me feel unwelcome."

The little one strutted up to Harry and stared right up at him, a cocky grin on his face. "Oh, you're welcome, honky—as welcome as a turd in a swimming pool."

The rest of the blacks laughed loudly.

"Now why don't you just turn around and get your white ass out of here," suggested the big one.

As the other black men started to move in on the two whites, Harry flashed his star.

"Cool it, dudes," advised Harry. "We're fuzz."

The little one nodded. "Well, now, ain't that nice? We know the law, man. You holding some kind of warrant?"

"What I'm holding is Henry Lee Caldwell."

"Never heard of him, honky. So why don't you just split on out of here before we get bugged."

"Abdul! Koblo!" A booming voice sounded behind the group crowding around Harry and Kate. The black men backed away and parted. An enormous, bullet-bald black man had entered silent and unnoticed. He was at least six feet five and weighed about two hundred and fifty pounds. He looked Harry and Kate up and down with eyes cold like rolled steel. "What's old Henry Lee been up to now?"

As the big man approached, Harry found himself, for the first time he could remember, talking up to someone. "He's been playing with dynamite. Which is a good way to get your fingers blown off."

The big man shrugged. "Life is full of risks."

"Are you Ed Mohamid?"

"That's right. So what's the trouble?"

"These honky pigs are looking for trouble," snorted the little one.

"We just want some information," replied Harry.

Mohamid nodded. "You have to learn to cool it, Abdul. I'll find out what they want." He nodded at an office at the back. "Come on back into my office." He pointed at Harry. "But just you."

Harry looked over at Kate, who was watching the crowd of young blacks around her apprehensively.

"Don't worry, pig," chuckled Abdul. "We'll see that she doesn't get lonesome."

"That's mighty white of you," said Harry. He followed Big Ed Mohamid into the office. Behind him, he could hear Kate saying:

"Now, gentlemen, before you do something rash, remember I am a police officer. If you touch me with the intent to do bodily harm, you are committing a felony, assaulting a police officer, and . . ."

Mohamid's office was decorated with African art. The big black man sank down into an ornately carved chair. He indicated a chair. "Sit down, Callahan."

Harry sat, surprised that Mohamid knew his name. "Where do I know you from?"

"You don't. I just know you." Mohamid swiveled around to a small bar built into the wall. "Little taste?"

Harry shook his head.

Mohamid picked up a bottle of bourbon and filled a glass. "As you can see, whites are not very popular around here. Especially the police." Mohamid took a drink. "So what's Henry Lee been up to?"

"You're telling me you don't know? Somehow I can't quite buy that."

"Nobody's selling it," retorted Mohamid easily. "He hasn't been around here for a long time."

"I thought he was a member in good standing."

"Not any more."

"What happened?" Harry wanted to know.

"He was a wild ass, is all. We have strict rules of

behavior here. Henry Lee started running around with some white cats with big ideas. And, like I said, we don't dig whitey around here. So finally he quit our association altogether. Why, did he do something foolish?"

"He was part of an outfit that ripped off the warehouse at Pier Fifty," Harry answered.

"Yeah. I heard about that."

"How?"

Mohamid grinned. "News gets around fast on the street. And I have a lot of sources."

"Maybe you know about it because you were in on it," suggested Harry seriously. "Three counts of murder. That's a heavy rap. You like to buy into that? Accomplice after the fact. Aiding and abetting?"

"Forget it, Callahan. You've got the wrong number. Me and my boys had nothing to do with that scene. We don't know anything about it. Besides, we're not into violence?"

"What are you into?"

"Waiting?"

"For what?"

Mohamid ran his palm across his shining scalp. "We're waiting for all you white assholes to blow each other away. We don't need to hurry it. You'll do it yourselves." He flashed his teeth. "Then we move in and take over."

"Sounds like a good system," said Harry. "Only don't hold your breath. We may hang in there longer than you think."

"Like I said, man, we can wait."

Harry leaned forward. "Tell me about Henry Lee and these white cats he was running around with. Do you know who they were?"

"Couple of dudes he knew from Vietnam were involved."

Harry took the list of names he had showed to McKay out of his pocket. "Any of these names grab you?"

Mohamid looked at the list. "Yeah," he admitted, "Bobby Maxwell. He was the leader."

"You know him?"

"A stone white bastard." He handed the paper back to Harry.

"Why do you say that?"

"He's the kind of dude who would cut his own mother's throat for five bucks. He used to be a pimp. They say he cut one of his hookers to pieces once just because she held out a couple of bucks on him. He was that way."

"Yeah," Harry said with a scowl. "I worked on the case. We never could pin it on anybody. Do you have any idea where I can find this dude?"

"I could check around," Mohamid offered. "But then, why should I? I mean, I'm not usually in the habit of helping the fuzz."

Harry understood the tone of voice. Mohamid was not going to give out any free information. He wanted something in return. A trade. "You scratch my back and I scratch yours. Is that it?"

"Something like that," admitted Mohamid. "One of our members was busted for cocaine possession. It was stupid—we don't allow our members to use drugs. But he's facing a stiff sentence. His name is Rosey Franklin. I can listen around the streets and get in touch with you if I hear something. And in return, you talk to the district attorney and see if you can get Rosey's charges reduced. Fair enough?"

Harry nodded. "I might do that. If the information is worth the time."

"Like I said, I've got a lot of sources. If I put out the word that I'm looking for Bobby Maxwell, I should have something back in a couple of days."

Harry stood up. "I need it real soon. And I don't want Maxwell to know that I'm looking for him. This it just between you and me."

"I can dig it."

Harry pulled a card out of his pocket and tossed it on the table. "You can get in touch with me at homicide. The number's on the card." He started for the door.

"You're on the wrong side, Callahan," said Mohamid suddenly.

Harry stopped, turned back. "How do you figure that one?"

Mohamid turned his big hands over, palms up. "You're out there on the street putting your ass on the line for a whole lot of dudes who wouldn't let you in their front door, any more than they would me. As far as they're concerned, you're just another pig, and they hate you for it."

"I'm not doing it for them," replied Harry quietly.

"Who, then?"

Harry opened the door. "You wouldn't believe me if I told you," he said as he went out.

Coming out of Mohamid's office, Harry found Kate surrounded by the young blacks, who were jiving with her.

"Come on, baby, don't be so uptight," chuckled one. He put his hand on her shoulder, then showed her the palm. "See? It don't rub off."

"Yeah, sweetheart," put in Abdul, "why don't you act a little more friendly? We're your friends."

Kate backed away, one arm outstretched to fend the group off, the other hand on the butt of her service revolver. "I want you all to back off," she demanded a little uncertainly. "Now, I'm not fooling around. You all know as well as I do that if I have to pull this piece, somebody is going to get busted."

"Ain't no need for that," argued Abdul coolly. "All we want to do is rap with you."

"Having fun, Inspector?" interrupted Harry. As he came forward, the blacks backed away slightly.

"Just getting acquainted," explained Abdul. "Like they say, man, get to know your local police."

Harry ignored him and stared at Kate. "Well, if you're through socializing, we have work to do."

Harry walked past her and through the group. Kate hurried after him.

"Come on back sometime, baby!" Abdul called after her. The other blacks erupted in a cackle of laughter.

"I'd like to know what you meant back there," Kate said as they came outside. "Because if you're trying to imply that I did anything to encourage that little exhibition, you are totally one hundred percent mistaken. I thought I handled the situation with professionalism."

Harry stopped in his tracks. "Look, Inspector, let's get something straight right now. I don't care what you do as long as it doesn't interfere with the job. As far as I'm concerned, you can go bang your head against the wall if that's what turns you on. It doesn't matter to me one way or the other. But I've got more important things to do than keep my eye on you and bail you out of trouble every five minutes. This may be some kind of game to you, but it isn't to me. It's my job."

"I'm perfectly capable of taking care of myself!" protested Kate angrily.

"Yeah," snorted Harry. "So I saw. You were doing real well back in there."

"Now just a damn minute—" Kate started.

"Shut up!" Harry ordered suddenly. As Kate opened her mouth to argue, he grabbed her and shoved her into a nearby doorway.

"What are you doing?" she demanded.

"Look," growled Harry, pointing. Kate followed his finger with her eyes. Down the street she saw a barricade of police cars blocking the street. She looked in the opposite direction. Another barricade blocked that intersection also. "What is it?" she asked.

"McKay," Harry growled. "He's convinced that black militants were behind the warehouse robbery. He must have gotten his search warrant. Now he's going to screw everything up!"

At that moment five police cars pulled past one of the barricades. They squealed to a stop in front of the *Uhuru* headquarters building. Men dressed in Tactical Squad gear began jumping out, ducking behind the cars for shelter. When they were finally set up, Captain McKay climbed out of the last car, carrying a bullhorn in one hand.

"All right, Mohamid!" McKay announced loudly. "This is Captain McKay of the San Francisco Police Department! I'm ordering you to throw down your weapons and come out peacefully now! You are completely surrounded! Come out with your hands raised over your heads!"

This said, McKay ducked back behind the protection of the car to wait. Dragging Kate after him, Harry scuttled across the street to where McKay was crouched.

"Callahan!" exclaimed McKay. "What the hell are you doing here?"

"Inspector Moore and I were just in there, talking to Mohamid," said Harry, dropping down beside McKay. "I'm convinced that they had nothing to do with that robbery."

"Well, I'm not. As far as I'm concerned, Mohamid is the man behind it."

"Look, Captain—"

"Dammit, Callahan," McKay roared, "I'm not asking for your opinion!"

Seconds later, the door to the *Uhuru* building opened. Mohamid walked out, hands held high. One by one, the rest of the members began to parade out. McKay dropped the bullhorn on the car hood and walked up to Mohamid.

"I'm placing you and your men under arrest," said McKay. He nodded to several of his men, who began handcuffing the *Uhuru* members.

Harry and Kate stood up. Mohamid looked around, saw Harry, and threw him an angry glare.

"Stupid goddamn brass asshole," muttered Harry. He headed for their car parked down the street. "Come on, let's go."

Kate watched the blacks being hustled into the waiting black-and-whites and then ran after Harry.

"What now?" she asked in the car.

"Back to homicide to wait for the shit to hit the fan."

Eleven

The foyer of the mayor's office was jammed with reporters and cameramen when Harry and Kate arrived. As they pressed their way through the knot of people, Harry spotted the mayor standing with Captain McKay and Lieutenant Bressler at the front of the crowd. McKay was beaming modestly, and the mayor stood poised with one hand on McKay's shoulder, in the manner of a man showing off a prize bulldog. In fact, the similarity between a bulldog and McKay was quite distinct, and the idea made Harry chuckle.

"What's funny?" Kate wanted to know.

"This." Harry waved his hand in an encompassing gesture. "It's such a circus."

"It's getting near election time," Kate reminded him. "You can't blame the mayor for wanting to make a few extra points with the voters. That's what politics is all about."

"I hate politics," Harry said. "I've never seen a politician yet who had any idea at all of what being a cop is all about. The only things they know how to do are raise taxes and screw up the government."

"Inspector Callahan," Kate said with mock severity, "you're such a cynic."

They continued to push forward until they managed to reach the front ranks of the crowd.

"As the mayor of San Francisco," the mayor was saying in his booming voice, "I would just like to make this official. Ladies and gentlemen of the press, this is one hell of a cop. I want you all to meet Captain Bradford McKay, the man responsible for breaking this difficult and dangerous case wide open. Bradford McKay!"

"Bullshit," murmured Harry.

The comment was lost in the clicking of cameras and popping of bulbs. The mayor flashed the winning smile he wore at all political events, showing rows of even, perfect teeth, which had cost him several thousand dollars and half a year of trips to the dentist. His smile broadened when he saw Harry and Kate standing off to one side.

"And here come a couple more!" The mayor nodded to his aide, Walter Martin, and whispered a few words to him. Martin nodded, walked over to Kate and Harry, and grabbed each firmly by an elbow.

"Right this way!" announced Martin loudly. "Here we are, ladies and gentlemen, the two officers who made the Caldwell arrest. Inspectors Harry Callahan and Kate Moore, two of San Francisco's finest."

Harry disliked the game-show manner that Martin had made his trademark over the years. As they walked into the center of attention, Harry engineered a stumble and brought his heel down hard on Martin's instep. The mayor's aide flinched, but managed to maintain his smile and bluff manner. Harry shrugged, then silently mouthed the word "sorry" in his direction. Martin shot him a withering glance.

"Boys," the mayor said to the press representatives, "how about getting one with me and Inspector Moore?" He shuffled himself around, pulling Kate toward him, posing next to her. He glanced over at Harry. "Callahan, why don't you get in this one, too?"

Harry stifled a groan as Martin pushed him up next to the mayor, who threw a friendly arm around his shoulder. Dozens of flashbulbs popped in Harry's face, reducing his vision to a sea of floating blue and red dots.

"Inspector Moore," he heard the mayor say, "is the first of her sex in the whole nation to become a full-time homicide investigator." He rearranged the pose for a photograph of just himself and Kate. "And I'd like to say right here and now that we're mighty proud of her stunning professionalism. I think her work on this case proves once and for all that a woman can do as good a job as any man, including as a police officer. Don't you agree, gentlemen?"

This last comment was directed toward McKay and Harry.

"Absolutely!" resounded McKay. Harry, however, declined to answer. He stood silent and scowling.

A few more photographs were taken at the mayor's request. When he was satisfied he had been photographed with everybody in every possible combination, he said, "Thank you all for your cooperation, ladies and gentlemen. It's always a pleasure to meet with you like this. Now, if you don't mind, I'd like to have just a moment alone with these fine police officers, and then we'll give the television people their chance."

The newspaper people moved off into the hall to wait, while the television cameramen and commentators began to set up their own equipment and lights. While all of this was going on, the mayor took the detectives aside.

"This is going to be fairly simple," the mayor explained quickly. "Just a few quick shots of me handing each of you a commendation for your performance." He looked around at his aide. "Walter, do you have those letters of commendation yet?"

Martin reached into his pocket and fished out several pieces of folded paper. "Right here, Your Honor. These are just some form *thank-you's*, but they'll do for the moment. Just so you have something to hand them in front of the cameras."

The mayor took the letters, not bothering to look at them. "Right. We'll get the real commendations out to you all in a few days," he assured the detectives. "This paperwork is killing me." He gave a hearty chuckle. "Now, here's how we'll handle it. First I'll introduce you, give you your commendations and a handshake, and then you'll move off—"

125

"To the left, out of camera range," Martin put in. "Just over by the wall."

"That's it," agreed the mayor. "Then I will take the opportunity to deliver a few well-chosen boots in the rear to those people who seem to feel that the police department has gone to hell in a handbasket under this administration."

There was a wave from the direction of the television crews. Someone held up two fingers. Martin nodded at the man.

"That means two minutes, Mr. Mayor," advised Martin.

"I know that," the mayor snapped. Then he smiled proudly at the four police officers. "Are we all ready? There's no reason to be nervous . . ."

"There's just one thing, Mr. Mayor," said Harry.

"Yes?"

Harry saw Bressler give him a warning look. He ignored it. "These letters of commendation we're going to get. What the hell are they supposed to be for?"

"Harry," Bressler tried to cut him off, "this is something that can wait until after the broadcast."

"The hell it can," Harry shot back.

McKay jumped in, flaring. "Watch it, Callahan. Remember, this is the mayor you're talking to."

Harry was not about to be silenced. "I just want to know what kind of shit we're shoveling here."

"It's quite all right," offered the mayor. "The inspector has a right to know what he's being commended for. I'm sorry, Callahan, but this all happened so suddenly that I didn't have time to brief you fully. I apologize."

Harry waited for his answer.

"Specifically," the mayor went on smoothly, "it's for your part in smashing a group of terrorists who were out to blackmail the city of San Francisco to the tune of two million dollars."

"Well, in that case you'd better forget it, because for your information, we didn't smash a goddamned thing!"

126

Harry's tone caught the mayor by surprise. "What is that supposed to mean?"

"Exactly what I said."

"But Mohamid and the members of *Uhuru* are behind bars. Caldwell was arrested in the act of planting a bomb in the Hall of Justice. As far as I'm concerned, the case is closed."

"Doesn't it bother anybody that we didn't find the rest of the dynamite, not to mention the guns or the ammunition or the LAWS rockets? We didn't find any weapons at the *Uhuru* headquarters. No one thinks that's important?"

"We'll find them," insisted McKay. "We'll get search warrants for the homes of all the *Uhuru* members. We'll probably find the stuff stashed in somebody's closet or buried in their basement. It's just a matter of time, now that we have the people behind it all."

"You're making one hell of a big mistake," Harry said. "*Uhuru* isn't involved in this. Caldwell hasn't been a member of that group for months. He was working for somebody else, some friends of his from Vietnam. Whoever they are, they're still running around out there. While we're standing around telling each other how smart we are, they're having a nice little horse-laugh, getting ready to blow hell out of this town."

McKay was furious. "All right, Callahan, that'll be enough of that. Cut it right there, or else. That's a direct order, Inspector."

Their loud voices were beginning to attract the attention of the television people, who were starting to stare with open interest.

Harry jabbed a thumb in the direction of the TV cameras. "Look, Mr. Mayor, you want to go over there and jerk everybody off, that's your business. If that's what gets you off, fine. But leave me out of it."

"That's it, Callahan," roared McKay. "I told you to shut your mouth. You just earned yourself a sixty-day suspension."

Harry was unruffled. "Make it ninety," he suggested with a calm smile.

"A hundred and eighty." McKay held out his hand. "Give me your star. Right now."

Harry pulled the badge out of his pocket and slapped it into McKay's outstretched palm. "Here you are, Captain. A six-pointed suppository."

McKay's face turned bright pink. "What did you say?" he demanded.

"I said shove it up your ass," Harry growled. "If you can find it." Harry spun on his heels and started for the door, pushing his way through the tangle of television newspeople.

Walter Martin hurried up to the mayor. "You're on, Mr. Mayor!"

The mayor watched with consternation as Harry vanished through the door. He thrust the extra folded commendation at Martin, then turned his brightest smile on Kate, McKay, and Bressler. If he was perturbed at the sudden turn of events, the mayor didn't show it. "All right, let's get this show on the road."

Kate looked at McKay with indecision. Suddenly she started for the door. "Excuse me, sir," she mumbled to the mayor, not waiting for an answer. She pushed past two women interviewers who were just coming toward her. Kate ignored their hurried questions and ran into the hall.

Harry was already starting down the stairs.

"Harry!" Kate called after him. "Wait a minute!"

Harry stopped halfway down the stairs, saw Kate running after him, and continued on down. By the time she finally caught up with him he had reached the door.

"Will you wait a second?" Kate demanded.

Harry stopped abruptly. "What's the matter?"

"Nothing. I just want to talk to you."

"Aren't you supposed to be up there with Mister Politics and the rest of the clowns, getting your letter of commendation? As often as you go to the bathroom, I thought you could use the paper." He straight-armed the door open and went out.

Kate came after him, galloping down the steps. "You never give up, do you?"

Harry started taking the steps two at a time. "Some-times," he muttered sourly.

"No, not you. Somebody else, maybe. But not you. You wouldn't know how to give up."

They reached the bottom of the steps. Harry paused again, looking at Kate with cold, hard eyes. "Look, I'm in a little bit of a hurry. I've got a lot of things to do. So if you've got something on your mind, why don't you go ahead and spill it all out?"

Kate bit her lip uncertainly. "I . . . I just wanted you to know that if there's anything that I can do, if there's anything you need—access to files and records—anything at all, just call me, and I'll get it for you. That's a promise."

Harry's look softened. He watched Kate's eyes for a long moment and then nodded slightly. "All right. I might just take you up on that."

Kate smiled happily. "Good. Any time. You know where you can call me."

"Yeah, right." Harry seemed to hesitate, wanting to say something, but not knowing quite how to say it. "I'll tell you something," he said finally.

"What?"

"Well . . . whoever draws you for a partner could do a whole lot worse."

"Thank you."

"Don't thank me," said Harry brusquely. "I mean, you've still got a lot to learn. But if you work hard, I think you might make it okay." He stopped, feeling awkward and foolish. "Aw, hell. You want to go someplace with me and get something to drink?"

"Okay," Kate replied. "How about a Coke?"

"A Coke. Yeah. Outstanding."

They drove to Golden Gate Park. Harry bought the Cokes at a refreshment stand outside the Museum of Fine Arts, getting them from an old man who had been working the same stand for as far back as Harry could remember.

Kate thanked him.

"You want to walk?" Harry asked.

Kate sipped through her straw, then nodded. "Sure, why not? I guess I'm off duty for the rest of the afternoon. His Honor probably had heart failure when both of us ran out on him like that."

"My heart bleeds for him."

They walked down one of the bridle paths toward the polo fields.

"You come here very often?" asked Kate.

"No, not really. I used to come here a lot with my wife." The lines in Harry's forehead etched deeper.

"I didn't know you were married." Kate's interest sounded more than simply professional.

"A long time ago."

"What happened?"

Harry searched for the briefest possible answer. "She was killed. In an automobile accident." His eyes had a faraway look, as if he was remembering every detail. There was no bitterness in his voice, only loss. "It was stupid, really. She was driving home. These guys in a pickup truck had been drinking. They went through a red light . . ." His voice trailed off.

"I'm sorry," said Kate.

They walked along in silence for a while.

"I was married, too," said Kate finally. "When I was sixteen. He was seventeen. We were just out of high school. We both thought we were in love. It lasted about six months, and one day we both realized we didn't want to spend the rest of our lives married to each other. So we got a divorce. No anger, no regrets. He sends me a Christmas card every year." She pursed her lips. "Funny. When we first got married, he was going to be an architect and I was going to be a lawyer. Now he's an insurance executive in Long Beach, and I'm a cop in San Francisco. I guess neither of us got what we wanted."

"You could still be a lawyer," Harry said.

"I've thought about it, believe me. To tell the truth, I'm not sure I want to be a lawyer any more. I see the way the courts work, and I say what's the use?"

Harry grinned. "That's pretty cynical. You sound like me.

They both laughed.

They continued on down the path to the polo field stables. Since it was a weekday, there was no game in progress. A couple of young boys were playing baseball on the field. Harry and Kate watched for a few minutes, then walked over to the stables to look at the horses.

"They're beautiful," said Kate, watching the groom brushing one of the animals down.

"You like horses?" Harry asked.

She nodded. "When I was a kid I used to go down to my aunt's ranch near Stockton. I'd ride bareback until I had sores on my butt." She chuckled, remembering. "Those were the best damned summers. I got thrown once and broke my leg in two places. As soon as the cast came off, I got right back on the same horse and rode him for the rest of the day, just to show him who was really the boss. I was a pretty stubborn kid."

"You still are," Harry added.

"Yeah, I know. So are you. We both are. Maybe that's why I like you."

At this last phrase, Harry suddenly seemed to tighten up.

Seeing this, Kate asked, "Did I say something wrong?"

Harry shook his head slowly. "No. It's just—I try not to get too friendly with partners."

"I know. I mean, I really do understand."

They continued walking. Finally Harry looked at his watch. "We better be getting back."

They turned around and started back.

"You ever go to the races?" Harry asked after a few moments.

"Do you?" Kate countered.

"I used to. Kind of got out of the habit, though." He shoved his hands in his pockets. "I was thinking that maybe you'd like to go out to Golden Gate Fields someday. I mean, if you've got the time."

131

"I'd like that a lot."

"How about next Saturday? Can you make it then?"

"Sure. It's a deal."

Twelve

It was the opening day of the season at windswept Candlestick Park. A near-capacity crowd of fifty-two thousand gathered to watch the Giants play the Houston Astros. As was the custom, the mayor was present for the opening ceremonies, tossing the first baseball while a dozen photographers captured the event on film for posterity.

The mayor hated baseball. He thought it was a stupid, dull game, and he disliked having to watch it. It never ceased to amaze him that people could get so excited about the game, standing in line for hours to get tickets, just so they could cram into rows of uncomfortable bleachers and watch a bunch of grown men hit a ball with a bat. It was ridiculous, and it was a waste of time.

It was necessary, of course, for him to stay for the game. It wouldn't do for His Honor to walk out in the middle of the first inning on opening day. No, he would have to sit through it all, smiling and cheering with the rest of the fools. A complete waste of time, but a part of his job.

By the end of the eighth inning the Giants were winning six to two. Montefusco was in fine form, keeping the Astros' hits to a minimum. The crowd loved it all.

Walter Martin turned to the mayor as the Astros came to bat at the top of the ninth. "We'd better get going if we want to beat the crowd, sir. It's almost four, and you have that City Council meeting at six. You'll just have time to look over your notes on the way if we leave now."

"Right you are, Walter," the mayor nodded gratefully. At least he wouldn't have to sit through the last part of the game and the closing ceremonies. Well, that was something, at any rate. As it was, he felt as if he would die of boredom. "Let's go."

The mayor said quick good-byes to the people around him, then he and Martin stood up and threaded their way through the cheering crowd.

Three fifty-eight.

Bobby Maxwell sat slumped in the driver's seat of a stolen Ford Econoline van which they had heisted from a downtown parking lot the previous night. Bobby watched the mayor's black Cadillac limousine parked in front of the main entrance. The limousine driver, a young cop in uniform, leaned against the fender of the car, arms folded, his cap pulled down low over his eyes to shade them from the bright sun.

Bobby heard a cheer from the stadium. He turned up the radio. Andrews had just hit another homer, bringing Cedeno home from second. That gave the Astros four.

Bobby shifted his gaze to the back of the van. Lalo was thumbing cartridges into a banana clip for an AR-15, while Karl was unwrapping a LAWS rocket. They went about their business with the professional skill of men trained in the use of weapons.

"Top of the ninth," Bobby told them. "He ought to be coming out pretty soon now, trying to avoid the crowd."

Lalo jacked the banana into the AR-15, cradling it lovingly in the crook of his arm. "I'm looking forward to this," he said, his voice edged with excitement. "It's going to be like the old days in 'Nam."

"I know what you mean," said Bobby. His voice was calm and emotionless. Unlike Lalo, Bobby never betrayed his feelings. You could never tell what was

134

going on in his mind. He was always so casual, even in the tightest situation. "This little caper goes down smooth, we're going to be home free for the rest of our lives."

"Two million dollars," Lalo whistled. "Man oh man oh man. It gives me a hard-on just thinking about all that money. I'm going to dig being rich. I've always wondered what it's like to be one of those wealthy fat-cats who can buy anything they want. Now I'm going to find out."

Bobby suddenly sat up straight and narrowed his eyes. The mayor and his aide were just coming out of the main entrance. The mayor said a few words to his driver, then climbed into the back seat of the waiting limousine. The aide got in next to him.

"Bingo," said Bobby. "Here we go." He turned off the ballgame on the radio.

"Soldier time," said Lalo. He flicked the safety off the AR-15, feeling the excitement within him begin to mount.

Bobby got out of the van and crossed to a pay phone ten feet away. He deposited a dime and dialed a number. It rang twice before there was an answer.

"Yeah?" It was Wanda's throaty voice.

"It's Bobby."

"So tell me, baby."

"The man is on his way."

"Beautiful."

"Everything set at your end?"

"We're in business."

"Okay. We're on our way."

"See you soon."

"You know it."

Bobby hung up the receiver and got back into the van. He watched the mayor's limousine pull through the parking lot toward the main gate. He waited until it was just driving out of the gate before he started the engine.

From the ballpark he could hear the cheers of the fans. Someone had just hit another run. Bobby smiled. It was as if they were cheering for him.

Three fifty-nine.

Wanda stood in a phone booth just inside the entrance to the Rupert Marine boatyard on Third Street. Through the entrance she could see the Third Street drawbridge which crossed the China Basin estuary.

She looked at her wristwatch. She knew it would take the mayor's limousine approximately ten minutes to drive the distance from Candlestick Park to the estuary. They had timed it twice yesterday.

Pulling her nun's cape around her, Wanda stepped out of the phone booth and walked to the pickup truck parked nearby. Tex sat slouched behind the wheel, drumming his fingers on the doorframe in rhythm with a Loretta Lynn tune on the radio.

"They're on their way," Wanda said.

"Good." Tex turned off the radio, then opened the glove compartment. Inside were two forty-five automatics. He lifted one out and handed it to Wanda through the window. She stuffed it under the folds of her cloak. The second forty-five Tex took for himself, checking the clip briefly, then cramming it into his belt where it settled firmly against his stomach.

"Remember," she said grimly, tapping his arm with one bright red fingernail, "when the bridge starts to raise."

"Uh-huh."

Wanda walked out of the boatyard entrance, crossing the street against the traffic. An oncoming car honked at her in annoyance. Wanda fought back the urge to flip the driver off. Instead she smiled piously at him as he slowed to let her pass. Frigging mother bastard, she thought.

The main control shack of the drawbridge was constructed on a raised metal framework to give the bridge operator a clear view of the estuary and the bay. Wanda clambered up the steep metal stairs to the control shack door, pulling the skirts of her habit up to keep from tripping over them. She hated the awkward, stuffy costume, and she felt ridiculous in

136

it. But it was a necessary part of Bobby's plan, and the irony of it was at least amusing to her.

At the top of the stairs Wanda knocked loudly on the shack door. Through the window she saw the bridge operator, about fifty-five, look up from some kind of report he was writing. He came to the door, unlatched it, and swung it open, looking at Wanda curiously.

"Hello, sister," he said affably. "How can I help you out?"

Wanda smiled meekly at him. "I wonder if you could do something for me?"

"Well, sure." His hand started to reach into his back pocket for his wallet. "How much do you want? Will five dollars be a big enough donation?"

"It's not money."

"No? What then?"

"What I want you to do is raise the bridge."

The bridge operator looked puzzled. Was she joking or what? He laughed. "Raise the bridge? Now, why on earth would you want me to do that?"

His smile disappeared as Wanda pulled the forty-five automatic out from under her cloak. "Because I say so, asshole," she snarled.

The operator's mouth dropped open in astonishment. "Now just hold on a minute—"

"Get back inside before I blow your fucking head off!" She jerked the gun at him menacingly.

The bridge operator hesitated only a second before deciding this was not a joke after all. "Okay, okay." He raised his hands and backed into the shack.

Wanda came into the control shack after him. She kept the automatic centered on the bridge operator's face. With her free hand she closed and latched the door behind her. She glanced at her watch again. Four oh-five. Another five minutes to wait, then things would really start popping. She smiled at the operator. He did not smile back.

Four-thirteen.

It took the mayor's car thirteen minutes to get from

137

the ballpark to Third and Army, which was just over a mile from the Third Street Bridge. An accident had slowed traffic to a crawl northbound. Impatient drivers were beginning to honk their horns angrily.

Bobby had maneuvered the van through the crowd of cars until it was directly behind the mayor's black Cadillac. They were behind schedule, he knew, but it would be all right. Stay calm and wait it out. Everything would work just like it was supposed to. Lalo came to the front of the van, peering through the windshield over Bobby's shoulder at the jammed traffic. "What's the hassle here?"

"Accident up ahead," explained Bobby calmly. "Looks like one car slammed into the back of another one. Traffic's backed up for quite a ways, it looks like."

"We're going to be late," Lalo complained. "It's already after four-ten."

"I know." Bobby was not in the least perturbed. A few minutes one way or the other wouldn't matter as long as Wanda kept her eyes open and played it smart. "Just keep cool, man," he advised Lalo. "We're going to make it." He nodded at the mayor's car ahead. "After all, the man is right here with us. Just keep thinking about all that money."

"Okay."

Ahead the black limousine pulled around the two smashed-up cars and began to pick up speed. Bobby could see the drivers of the damaged vehicles arguing about whose fault it was. He eased past the scene of the accident, then floored the accelerator and roared off after the mayor's car.

Four-sixteen.

Where the hell were they? Wanda studied the dial of her watch nervously. The mayor's limousine was late. Bobby was late. She looked out of the window at the traffic along Third Street moving toward the bridge. There was no sign of the limousine or of the stolen van. What had happened? Had something gone wrong? Bobby had told her not to panic in case there was some kind of delay. She was to wait until four-thirty. If the limousine did not show by then, she was to kill the bridge operator, join Tex in the pickup truck, and get the hell out of there. But not until four-thirty. There was still plenty of time. Fourteen minutes left. She was certain the limousine would show. It had to. It just had to.

"Hey, lady, what's all this about, anyway?" It was the bridge operator. He was getting impatient. His initial fear of Wanda and her gun had begun to wear off.

"You just shut your fucking mouth, pops," Wanda told him harshly. She watched his fat, sweating face with a feeling of revulsion. She was going to enjoy killing him when the time came, regardless of whether or not the mayor showed up. The old fart, he deserved to die.

She continued to watch the street.

Four-eighteen.

In his air-conditioned limousine the mayor was sitting back, enjoying the ride. He liked driving through San Francisco. Hell, he was the mayor after all, wasn't he? It was his city. Why shouldn't he enjoy it?

"Okay, Walter," he said to his aide, "tell me about this City Council meeting tonight."

Martin opened his briefcase and took out a handful of papers. He began to go over the mayor's notes.

The mayor listened to him drone on only half attentively, his eyes focused in the middle distance. There were other things on his mind. Right now he was thinking about the future. His future. It was all right being mayor, of course, but he aspired to bigger things. Next year he would run for governor. Why not? It was something he had been turning over in his mind for some time now. He would announce his candidacy in the spring. Given the right amount of party support he was almost certain he could win. Governor of the State of California. Now that would really be something. And after that . . . well, who could say? He wasn't so old that he couldn't go on from there. Why, there might even be the possibility of a presidential nomination in there if he played his cards right. It was certainly something to think about.

Glancing sideways out of the back window he saw a blue van behind them, following closely. The mayor frowned thoughtfully. He was sure he had seen the same van pull out of the Candlestick parking lot just after they had left. Of course, it was probably just a coincidence. Or another van. There had to be hundreds just like that in San Francisco. Still . . .

"Dave?" The mayor cut in on Martin's briefing, leaned forward, and tapped the driver on the shoulder.

"Yessir?"

"That blue van behind us. Isn't he following us a little close?"

The driver checked his rear-view mirror. "Yessir, he is at that. I'm trying to let him pass." He stuck his arm out of the window, motioning the van past. It stayed where it was.

"Looks like he doesn't want to go around us," said Martin, looking through the back window. He put the bond issue papers back into the briefcase. The mayor hadn't really seemed interested, anyway. If he wanted to be caught flat-footed in front of the City Council, that was his problem. He, Martin, tried to do his job properly, but sometimes it was very difficult.

"Probably just a lousy driver," decided the mayor. He hoped that was all it was. He was surprised to find that it worried him. He had been working too hard lately, that was it. What he needed was a couple of days off. Some time out on the old golf course. A chance to relax.

Cheered by the thought, he settled back once more and closed his eyes. Maybe he could get in a little nap before that damned meeting.

Four-nineteen.

Wanda saw the mayor's limousine coming, four blocks away, closely followed by the blue van. There did not seem to be any problem. Maybe they had just slowed down in the traffic. Whatever the delay had been, everything would be all right now. They were here.

She turned to the bridge operator, thrusting the automatic into his soft stomach. He started fearfully. She saw it in his eyes, and it pleased her. "Raise the bridge," she ordered. "Right now."

The operator was slow in moving. Wanda watched him impatiently, then rapped the barrel of the gun against the side of the man's skull. He cried out as a streak of blood appeared at his temple. He clutched at his bleeding head and stumbled backwards. He nearly fell, but caught onto the switchboard console for support.

"I said now, I mean now," Wanda snarled. "You better get your ass in gear, pops, and hurry it up."

The bridge operator pressed a button and began pulling a series of levers. At the bridge intersection Wanda saw the signal light flash red. A striped wooden arm swung down horizontally, blocking the oncoming traffic. A warning bell began to ring in timed rhythm with the red light.

"Look, lady," said the operator fearfully, "I don't know what this is all about, and I really don't care. I'll do whatever you say for me to do." He wiped the beading sweat from his forehead. "Just don't shoot me, okay?"

Wanda was not in the mood to be polite. "If you don't shut up, I will shoot you. Just keep your goddamn face front."

The van was still following closely, refusing to pass. Ahead the mayor saw the Third Street bridge start to rise. The street was blocked off in front of them, and the van was blocking them behind. He didn't like it. He didn't like it at all.

"There's something funny here, Dave," he told the driver. "I don't like it."

"Neither do I," the policeman answered.

"Take a right at the corner and go down Amador."

The driver nodded and started to turn.

"Why do you think they're following us?" asked Martin nervously.

The mayor did not answer. There could be any number of reasons—and all of them were frightening.

As the limousine started to turn, a pickup truck suddenly burst out of a driveway, cutting them off at the corner, blocking the turn. At the same time the van roared up on the left side.

"Dave!" shouted the mayor. "Get me out of this!"

The driver jammed the gas pedal to the floor, spinning the wheel. The limousine squealed in front of the van, which hit its brakes hard. As the mayor's car tried to pull around the van, Bobby suddenly rammed it hard. The limousine teetered on two wheels, then overturned.

Behind them a big truck and trailer squealed to a halt. The driver, a big, muscular black man, jumped out of the cab with a tire iron in his hand.

Bobby threw open the van door and climbed out.

"What the hell's going on here?" demanded the truck driver angrily.

Bobby whirled on him, dragging a gun out of his jacket. He fired point-blank at the driver, shooting him in the face. The driver skidded back across the pavement, dead.

At the same time Tex jumped out of the pickup truck. The driver of the mayor's limousine was just climbing through the window of the overturned car. He staggered to his feet. Seeing Tex rushing at him, he pulled out his service revolver. Tex fired twice from the hip. The policeman was slammed back against the limousine.

The back doors of the van burst open. Lalo jumped out, armed with one of the M-16s, while Karl carried the LAWS rocket.

Bobby pointed past the stopped truck and trailer. "Block off Third Street!" he ordered.

Karl nodded and quickly set up the rocket launcher. A station wagon approached up Third, a man and two children inside. Karl took aim and fired. The station wagon exploded in a mushroom of flame, pieces of burning metal and bodies showering the street, blocking it.

Bobby hurried to the other side of the limousine and dragged the back door open. Inside the mayor and Martin stared up at him with terrified faces.

"Let's go!" Bobby shouted, waving his automatic.

"Where?" demanded Martin.

Bobby grinned savagely. "Not you, sweetlips," he snarled. He jammed the gun in Martin's face and fired, blowing the top of the aide's head off. The body flopped back into the limousine, spattering the mayor with blood. The mayor recoiled in horror.

"Out, you son of a bitch!"

"No! What kind of people are you?"

Bobby reached in, grabbed the mayor by the shirtfront, and dragged him out of the car. He slammed him up against the side of the limousine, then pistol-whipped him across the mouth with the hot barrel of the automatic. Blood filled the mayor's mouth, and he felt one of his hand-tooled teeth snap off at the gumline.

Tex appeared at Bobby's side. He and Bobby grabbed an arm each and hauled the mayor across the street toward the boatyard. Lalo and Karl followed.

In the bridge control shack Wanda had watched it all take place. She was grinning from ear to ear. Bobby was a genius, a goddamn genius. It had all worked exactly as he had said it would. And the rest of it would work, too. They were going to be rich, and there was no one who could stop them.

"You dirty bastards!" growled the bridge operator, anger replacing his fear. He took a step toward Wanda, his teeth bared in open hatred. "You filthy murdering scum!"

Wanda fired twice at close range into his stomach. With a stunned look the operator collapsed on the floor, clutching his stomach. He was not dead. He stared up at Wanda, his lips moving trying to say something but unable to speak.

Wanda aimed carefully and shot him again, this time through the head.

Tex dragged the mayor down the dock to the motorboat tied there, shoving him aboard. The mayor stumbled and fell to the deck in a terrified heap. Blood trickled from his battered mouth.

"Get your ass below," Tex ordered, gesturing sharply with his gun.

The mayor crawled across the deck to the companionway. He went down them as quickly as possible, into the cabin.

Behind Tex, Bobby climbed aboard, followed by Lalo and Karl. Bobby climbed up to the cockpit. He punched the starter switch. The boat engine sputtered, then rumbled smoothly to life.

"Where the fuck is Wanda?" Bobby wanted to know.

"She's coming," said Lalo, nodding to the pier. "She's right behind us."

Wanda came running through the boatyard gate, her skirts held high. She jumped onto the boat.

"Goddamn these things!" she swore, dragging the nun's habit up over her head. "I could hardly move!" She tore the costume off and threw it onto the deck. Underneath she was wearing Levi's and a tight T-shirt.

"Cast off!" called Bobby.

Tex jumped onto the dock to untie the stern line. Lalo climbed forward and cast off the bow. Bobby waited as Tex jumped back aboard, then gunned the engine. The boat roared away from the dock, down the estuary, headed for the bay.

Behind it, the smoke from the blazing station wagon filled the sky.

Thirteen

By six o'clock it was the biggest news story of the year. The mayor of San Francisco had been kidnapped. Snatched off the street in broad daylight, while driving home from the opening day at Candlestick Park. Seven people had been brutally murdered in the process of the kidnapping, two of them children under ten years old. The kidnappers had been armed with machine guns and bazookas. Four men and one woman. They were still at large, armed, and very dangerous.

Within hours every member of the police department had been called back to duty. Everyone available was working on the case. The chief himself was taking personal charge of the investigation. The biggest dragnet in the history of San Francisco was being pulled across the city. The F.B.I. and the California Highway Patrol were cooperating fully. Every known radical, militant, dissident, and malcontent in the police files was dragged in off the streets and questioned. Any lead, no matter how vague, was investigated and followed to the ground. It was impossible that the kidnappers could long evade the arm of the law with such an army of police concentrating on finding them. Early arrests were predicted and made, but none were the right people.

The reporters and politicians had a field day with the story. The governor called it a shocking example

145

of the moral decline of our society and demanded more stringent gun legislation. The mayor of Los Angeles revealed that he too had received kidnap threats and was under twenty-four hour police protection. The Vice President used it as an excuse to launch into a tirade against those who would undermine the very freedom they were pretending to protect. Howard K. Smith considered it ironic that such an incident should occur during America's Bicentennial celebration. The Berkeley *Barb* applauded it as a right-on example of the revolutionary spirit of the people, vowing that the struggle against the fascist oppressors would never end. The *New York Times* ran a long editorial which came to no conclusion whatsoever.

Everyone was having a hell of a good time with it, with the exception of the overworked police department, many of whom had visions of vanishing jobs and lost pensions. They all knew that when this was all over, heads were going to roll. Some began looking around for someone else to point the finger at, should it begin to point at them.

The next day dawned and grew old without any sign of the kidnappers—or the mayor. The massive police investigation had turned up no concrete clues as to who was behind the plot, why they had done it, or where they had vanished to. The crime rate in the Bay area, however, dropped markedly; due to the excessive zeal with which the police staged their manhunt, most of the criminal faction had gone hastily underground to wait for the heat to blow over.

It was suggested darkly by the media that the kidnappers had left the state, perhaps even the country. Reports that they had been seen flooded in from across the country. Eyewitnesses spotted a man resembling the mayor being accompanied by several suspicious persons into a motel near Bakersfield. At practically the same time a young woman saw him in a drugstore in Las Vegas, a married couple spotted him in a station wagon in Seattle, and a grocery store owner in Phoenix sold him a roll of toilet paper. There was even a report from Florida, where several people were certain they had seen the mayor boarding a small private plane. The pilot had spoken with a distinct Cuban accent.

Privately the police admitted they hadn't the slightest idea where the kidnappers had gone. Publicly, however, they had several important leads they were following up and expected a break in the case any time now.

Then the tape came.

A telephone call to an underground San Francisco radio station from a woman explained that a tape cassette had been left in a phone booth across the street, listing the demands of the People's Revolutionary Strike Force. The tape was found and played on the air. The kidnappers wanted two million dollars in exchange for the mayor's safe return. The police would be contacted as to the place and time of the delivery. Instructions were to be followed exactly. Otherwise the mayor would be returned in individually wrapped pieces.

The police descended upon the radio station and spirited the tape away with them, but not before a copy had been bootlegged for sale to other stations. Meanwhile, a special meeting between the police chief, the city council, and the mayor's family took place. Arrangements to raise the two million dollars were made.

It was an old apartment building on Jackson near Russian Hill. Once it had been an attractive Victorian house, but the years had changed all that. Now, like so many other San Francisco structures, it was only a faded memory of the city's past glory.

Standing in the dimly lit entrance hall of the building, Captain McKay struck a match and peered at the names on the mailboxes. "I don't see his name. Maybe he moved," said McKay at last. He shook out the match just before it could burn his fingers.

"No, this is it," replied Lieutenant Bressler. "I've been here a couple times. And he hasn't moved. He just took his name off the mailbox. He says nobody

147

writes to him anyway. All he gets is junk mail."

The front door opened. A landlady with the face of an owl poked her head out suspiciously. "What do you want?" she demanded in a shrill voice.

"Harry Callahan," McKay told her.

"What about him?" She tugged the neck of her frayed bathrobe tightly around her neck.

McKay showed her his star. "Police. We're looking for him. It's important."

The landlady apparently didn't think much of the policeman's badge. She sniffed contemptuously. "How come he got thrown off the cops?"

"He didn't get thrown off," Bressler said. "He's only suspended, pending a hearing."

She sniffed again. "Suspended, thrown off. It's all the same."

"No, it's not the same—"

"It is so, young man!" The landlady was in no mood to be disagreed with.

"Do you know where we can find him?" asked McKay.

"I might."

There was a silence.

"Well, would you mind telling us? We'd appreciate any help you can give us."

She looked McKay up and down, as if she was considering paying a down payment on him. "Try Kelly's on Divisadero. It's a pool hall. He goes there sometimes."

McKay started to thank her, but before he could get a word out, the landlady closed the door sharply in his face.

"Not very friendly," McKay commented as they started down the front steps.

Bressler shrugged. "Why do you think he lives there?"

Shooting pool was one of the few games Harry Callahan really enjoyed, primarily because it was something he could do alone. Team sports or group games held no appeal for Harry. He seldom shot pool with anyone else. Instead he preferred to pit himself against the table, making his own luck, winning or losing on his own skill.

Tonight his game was off. He had missed two shots in a row, and, although they were not easy shots, they were ones he should normally have made. His concentration was bad, that was the problem. He was preoccupied . . .

The portable color television perched on the front counter was turned up loud. 'The owner, rather than watching it, had fallen asleep in his chair. The six o'clock news was on, and the newscaster was talking about the kidnapping. There were no new developments; the police had extended their dragnet to include Alameda and Contra Costa counties; the chief was confident the mayor would be returned safely. In other words, nobody knew anything. There was no mention of the ransom demand or whether the kidnappers had yet set up a time and place for the delivery.

"Hello, Harry."

Harry looked up from his shot to see Bressler and McKay standing by the table. He was not surprised to see Bressler, having expected him to show up eventually. McKay was something else again. It had to be important for McKay to come looking for him.

Harry bent back over the table to line up his next shot. Without looking at either man he said, "What can I do for you two?"

Bressler gave Harry a lopsided grin. "We'd like to talk to you."

"You are talking to me." He dropped the six ball neatly into a corner pocket.

McKay cleared his throat. "We'd like your attention," he said. His voice had a brittle edge to it.

Harry came around the table so his back was to McKay. "I'm listening," he said, his voice holding no interest at all.

McKay began to turn red, but he held himself in check. It wouldn't do to start arguing right off. "I want all the information you have on the mayor's kidnapping."

"Why would I have any information on that?"

"Let's not bullshit each other. We all know that you're interested in this case because these are the guys who killed Frank DiGeorgio. I know you, Callahan. You're not going to sit around on your ass and let them get away with it."

"I'm not? You don't seem to remember that I'm still on suspension." Harry shot again, dropping the three in the corner and the nine in the side. "Why don't you guys go away and let a private citizen enjoy some peace and quiet?"

"Harry, we know that you've been asking around on the street," said Bressler. "You put the word out that you want something on the people who snatched the mayor. We want to know if you've come up with anything yet."

Harry straightened, putting the butt of the cue on the floor. He fixed his eyes on McKay. "I thought you already had the guys. Black militants, you said. Your fabulous police instincts, remember? Ed Mohamid and his boys. As I recall, you even got a commendation for your brilliant detective work. What can I tell you, super-cop?"

McKay glowered. There was an uneasy silence. "All right, Callahan. I . . . I was wrong," he admitted, having trouble getting the words out through his clenched teeth.

Harry was unmoved by the admission. "I know you were. But it's real nice to know that even you realize it. I guess it's because you're a trained policeman. So you were wrong. Suppose you go and tell that to the seven people those bastards killed. Maybe we can put it on their gravestones: 'Captain Bradford McKay was wrong and he's sorry.' That should make them all feel a whole lot better."

"If you've got any information, Callahan, I want it. I want to know what your snitches told you."

"I'll handle this one my way—and that doesn't include telling you one goddamn thing."

"Dammit, Callahan, we play as a team!"

150

Harry chuckled grimly. "The last time we played as a team, I got the bat stuck up my ass."

McKay was livid. "I can make you talk, Callahan!"

"You could try," said Harry. "I'd like to see you try."

McKay pushed his face close to Harry's. "In that case you listen good. I'm ordering you to stay out of this case. We don't want you butting in and screwing things up for us."

"I'd say you already did that on your own, Captain. How can I compete with the best fuck-up in the business?"

McKay stayed in control. "The negotiations with the kidnappers are at a crucial point right now. You could wreck it all by doing something rash on your own."

Harry stared at McKay darkly. "You mean to tell me that you intend to pay those bastards off? You're really going to hand over two million dollars and let them go? I don't believe it! You can't be serious."

"The mayor's family is loaded," said Bressler. "They can afford to pay it."

"To hell with the money! What about all the people they killed? The cops? Those kids in the station wagon? Those gas company guys? Isn't murder against the law any more?"

McKay clenched his fists in contained anger, the knuckles turning white. "Murder isn't the issue here. The safe return of the mayor is what's important. I'm telling you to stay out of it."

"What you're really telling me," Harry countered, "is that you're willing to turn the world over to these punks. What the hell is it all coming to, anyway? Anyone who's got balls enough to take a hostage can do anything he wants to and walk out the door. If these assholes get away with it this time they'll do it again. And they'll keep on doing it. And so will others, until somebody tells them it won't work."

"I want you to stay out of this case!" McKay shouted, unable to contain himself any longer. "And if I hear anything to the contrary you're finished as a cop in San Francisco. You step out of line so much as an inch, I'll have your ass in jail for obstructing justice and anything I can think of!"

Harry carefully put the cue down across the green table. "I'd like to make one statement."

"Go ahead," snarled McKay.

"Your mouthwash isn't getting the job done."

With that Harry walked out of the pool hall.

It was a bright, sunny day in Golden Gate Park. Harry sat on a bench near Stow Lake, watching a squirrel sniff cautiously at a half-eaten peanut butter sandwich someone had dropped. The squirrel contemplated the sandwich for a moment before finally scampering off in search of something else.

Harry saw the big black man coming down the path toward him, immediately recognizing the distinctive bald head of Big Ed Mohamid. Today Mohamid was dressed in a flashy white suit, a brightly colored handkerchief hanging out of his breast pocket.

Mohamid plopped his big bulk down onto the bench beside Harry. "Hear you been trying to get ahold of me. I'm liable to get a bad name."

"Tell them I'm sweet on you," Harry suggested.

"So what can I do you for?"

Harry hung his elbows over the bench back. "Information. I want a line on the bastards who grabbed the mayor."

Mohamid's big mouth split into a wide grin. "You don't ask for much, do you? What makes you think I should know ?"

"Like you said before, you've got sources. I figure if anybody knows something, you do."

"Maybe," Mohamid admitted. "But why should I help you? I hear you're suspended. You can't scratch my back any more. And I sure as hell don't owe you pigs anything. 'Specially after you busted us."

"That wasn't me. That was McKay."

Mohamid cocked his head. "Yeah, I'm going to remember that ofay. He is definitely on my shit list."

"He's on a lot of shit lists."

"So I repeat, why should I help you, Callahan?"

152

"Because if you don't," Harry said matter-of-factly, "I'll let it get out that you're a snitch."

Mohamid watched Harry without amusement. "Don't say that, man. Not even as a joke."

Harry's face was serious. "Who's joking?"

Mohamid studied Harry. Suddenly he burst out in a booming laugh. "You really are a dirty bastard, aren't you, Callahan?"

"The dirtiest."

"Yeah, well, I'll keep it in mind." His eyes twinkled as he watched Harry. "Okay, I'll tell you what I know. It's not much, but maybe you can use it."

"Shoot."

Mohamid dragged the colorful silk handkerchief out of his pocket and mopped it across his perspiring bald head. "Word is around that one of Bobby Maxwell's old chicks has been running around with some of these cats calling themselves the People's Revolutionary Strike Force. The way I hear it, she was the chick involved in the grab."

"You know her name?"

"Wanda. I don't know her last name. I don't even know if Wanda is her real name, but that's the one she uses. And I'll tell you something else, too. This 'People's Revolutionary' thing is all a shuck. These cats don't give a shit for the people. They're in it for the bread. The two million, that's what they want. The revolutionary hype was Bobby Maxwell's idea. He figured he could get some support from the militants that way. When it's all over, they're going to take the cash and split the country."

"This Wanda chick. Where do I find her?"

"Last I heard, she worked at this massage parlor down in North Beach, just off Broadway. A place called the Doll's House. One of those places where they let you hump yourself for fifty bucks, you know? Anyway, she's a big, tall brunette. And a pro. She worked the streets as one of Maxwell's hookers for a couple of years. Funny thing is, except for him, she doesn't dig guys. She prefers other chicks."

"That it?"

"That's what I know."

Harry rose. "Okay. Thanks for the talk. Maybe I can return the favor sometime."

"I'll let you know."

"Take it easy." Harry started off up the path toward the parking lot where he had left his car.

"Hey, Callahan!"

Harry turned back.

Mohamid gave him a parting grin and a clenched fist salute. "Keep cool, dude!"

Fourteen

The Doll's House was a second story walk-up just off Broadway, conveniently located over a porno movie theater. A multicolored door, decorated in cheap fluorescent paints that had long ago lost their brilliance, led to a steep, narrow, lightless stairway which vanished upwards around a sharp turn. A cardboard sign was thumbtacked to the door, upon which someone had printed LEARN THE LOVE TUSSLE.

Harry, dressed in well-worn Levi's and an old leather jacket, read the announcement with a wry grin. The "Love Tussle"? Well, that was a new way to advertise what they meant without creating any legal complications. Over the years he had seen that statement made in a variety of codes: do-it-yourself photography, nude encounter sessions, sex therapy. It all meant the same thing. Come in and get laid.

Harry trotted up the stairs, coming around the dark bend to find himself in a waiting room not much wider than the stairs. It was done in red-and-white stripes like a candy cane and decorated with cast-off furniture. The thick smell of cheap perfume hung in the stale air. The light in the room was little better than that on the stairs, resembling a kind of murky twilight.

A bleached blond in short-shorts and halter top came through a beaded curtain at the back of the room. She was long past thirty, with fat hips and thighs and bulging breasts. She smiled at Harry coquettishly.

"Hi there. My name is Jenny. What's the matter, guy? Cat got your tongue?"

"This is the Doll's House?" asked Harry suspiciously. In truth, the place looked more like a condemned barber shop than a massage parlor.

"Like it says on the door, honey. Come on in. Come right on in and enjoy yourself. We got a lot to offer a guy who looks as cute as you do."

"Uh-huh." Harry stuck his hands in his pockets and pushed his face into an expression that he hoped suggested extreme stupidity. "My brother was up here last week," he said slowly. "Tall fella, blond hair, going bald? Name's Bradford McKay. Maybe you remember him?"

"Oh, sure I remember him," nodded Jenny. It was obvious from her blank look that she couldn't remember the face of the last guy to come through the door.

Harry opened his mouth and pointed to his front teeth. "He has a gold tooth in front, right here. You couldn't miss it."

"That's him." She moved closer to Harry, slipping her arm through his, snuggling her hip against him. "You know what I bet you'd like, slick? I bet a big guy like you would like to learn how to do the love tussle."

"Yeah, that sounds real swell. But . . . uh . . . what I'm really looking for is this certain girl. My brother said she was real—you know, talented."

"We've got a whole bunch of girls here, slick. And all of them are warm and willing." She began to toy with the buttons of Harry's shirt. He assumed she was trying to turn him on.

"Her name is Wanda," Harry confided.

"You can have anybody you want."

"Well, she's the one I want. Like I told you, my brother thinks she's fantastic."

"Right." Jenny leaned closer conspiratorially. "Listen, honey, can I trust you?"

Harry gave her his best dumb look. "Sure. What is it you want to tell me?"

"To get all this special, personal treatment it costs you seventy-five dollars."

"Seventy-five bucks? That's a little steep, isn't it? My brother told me it only cost fifty—"

"Of course," she cut him off, "that includes the works."

Harry blinked at her. "The works?"

"Yeah, the works. You know?"

"No."

Jenny looked at the ceiling briefly. "Jesus . . ." She lowered her voice. "We're not supposed to do this, because the heat's been giving us a real hard time lately, but seeing as how your brother was here, I guess I can trust you." She looked around to see if anyone was listening. "The seventy-five bucks includes personal instructions from the girl of your choice in thirty-two different and exotic positions of lovemaking. Now you know what I mean?"

Harry bobbed his head dully. "Oh. Oh, yeah." He wrinkled his forehead. "Thirty-two ways, huh? I didn't know you could do it thirty-two different ways."

"Then, slick, you have definitely come to the right place. We can teach you things you never even imagined."

"Sounds good," Harry admitted.

The beaded curtain at the back of the room parted again, and a big man in a T-shirt stepped through. The bouncer, Harry figured. He looked at Harry with the seeming intelligence of a woolly mammoth.

"That'll be seventy-five dollars cash," said Jenny, her tone suddenly becoming very businesslike. The bouncer's entrance was apparently her cue to hurry the john along. "You pay me first."

Harry took a wad of bills out of his pocket and peeled off the right amount of currency. Jenny took the money, putting it into a cigar box in the desk drawer.

"Right this way," she told Harry. The bouncer moved aside. Jenny pushed through the beaded curtain. Harry followed her down a long hallway lined with doors. They went into a small room.

"Here we are, slick."

Harry stared around the room. There was a narrow bed in the corner. On the bed was a life-sized inflated female doll. As Harry moved closer he saw that some highly imaginative artist with colored felt-tip pens had given the doll nipples and pubic hair. A matted wig draped over the rubber head completed the effect of absurdity.

"What's that?" Harry asked, indicating the rubber figure.

Jenny shrugged. "You've heard of a tackling dummy like football players use? Well, this is the same principle."

"That's the big thrill? For seventy-five bucks I get to make it with an inflated rubber dolly?"

"Thirty-two ways, don't forget," she pointed out.

"You must be kidding. This is nothing but a big rip-off. Even if I was nuts enough to do it, you're the one that would have to pay me for a show like that."

The big bouncer appeared in the doorway. He sneered at Harry with a wash of contempt. "You got any objections, creep?" he demanded in a deep, threatening voice designed to terrify dissatisfied customers.

Harry gave a meek little smile and shook his head quickly. "Uh . . . no. Just wondering."

Jenny headed for the door. "Just take off your duds, slick. I'll send her right in."

The bouncer chuckled. "Have fun, sport."

Jenny and the bouncer vanished, leaving Harry alone. He went over to the bed and gave the rubber doll a poke. The wig fell off, and Harry saw that the same artist had drawn a face on, as well. It stared up at Harry with wide blue eyes and bright red lips.

The door to the room opened. A girl entered, wearing a string bikini which barely concealed her ample proportions and smoking a cigarette. She was kind of cute, but her blond hair and short stature told Harry she was definitely not Wanda.

"Hi there," she said as if talking to a door.

"You're not Wanda," Harry told her.

"Yeah? Well, those are the breaks, honey." She crossed to the bed, picked up the doll, and shook it. "Your girl friend here needs air. You can't hump a limp dummy, I always say. I ought to know, I've tried it often enough." She chuckled, amused by her own humor. She saw that Harry was not amused and glanced at him critically. "And speaking of limp dummies, don't you think you better take your clothes off? You only bought yourself half an hour, kiddo."

She put the cigarette down, sat on the edge of the bed, and started blowing up the dummy through a nozzle in the foot.

"Where's Wanda?" Harry demanded. "I asked for Wanda."

The girl stopped blowing. "Beats hell out of me, Tom," she said indifferently. "I just work here. If it's going to make you feel any better, you can call me Wanda, okay? You can call me anything you want— momma, King Kong, even horseshit. I don't care. It's your seventy-five bucks, right? Whatever turns you on, honey. Do your own thing, as they say."

She started blowing on the dummy again. Harry picked up her cigarette and pressed the glowing tip against the doll. It popped with a loud bang. The girl jumped, startled. She flung the rubber doll on the floor angrily. It took a second for her to regain her composure, then she stood up, fists on her hips.

"What the hell did you do that for?" she growled. "That's going to cost you, hotpants. Those dummies cost twenty-five bucks apiece."

Harry reached out, grabbed the girl by the hair, and jerked her toward him. He pushed her up against the wall and held her there, pushing his face within a few inches of her own.

The girl was terrified. "If I scream," she managed to whisper, "Hughie will come in here and tear you apart."

"I'm asking you one more time, little girl," Harry said softly. "Where's Wanda?"

The girl swallowed. "I don't know, man. Honest, I

don't know. I'd tell you if I did. But she left here a couple of weeks ago. She doesn't work here any more."

Harry tightened his grip on her hair. "How can I find her?"

"Ask Buchinski," she suggested quickly. "He's the guy who owns this place."

"Where is he?"

"He's got an office in the back."

Harry let go of her hair. "No screams," he told her. "Or I'll come back in here and use your empty little head for a football." He turned and strode out of the room, while the girl stood frozen against the wall.

Harry made his way down a maze of corridors toward the back of the building. Entering a large room at the end of the hall, he found an astonishing sight. Twenty or thirty old ladies were seated at two long tables. In front of each was a stack of blue stationery and a cup full of lipsticks. The old ladies were all writing on the stationery in longhand, copying a message printed in block letters on a blackboard at one end of the room. Harry squinted at the message and read:

DEAR LOVER,
MY NAME IS INGRID. MY ROOM MATE AND I HAVE COME FROM DENMARK TO CALIFORNIA TO GET INTO THE MOVIES. WE HAVE HAD SOME BAD LUCK, SO WE MADE A RED-HOT MOVIE TOGETHER, AND WE WOULD LIKE TO SEND YOU A COPY OF THIS COLLECTOR'S ITEM FOR ONLY FIFTY DOLLARS.
LOVE AND KISSES,
INGRID

Harry stared at the message incredulously, then looked back at the old ladies copying it down. In a moment one of the women finished writing. She painted her lips with lipstick and then planted a big red kiss on the bottom of the letter. Putting the finished letter aside, she took another piece of stationery and began to write again.

"Excuse me, lady," Harry asked the old woman nearest to him. "How much do you get paid to do this?"

"A dollar fifty an hour," she told him with a bright, grandmother smile.

"But that's not even the minimum wage."

Her brow wrinkled solemnly. "Have you ever tried to live on Social Security, sonny?" she asked.

"No," he admitted.

"Well, don't knock it, then," she snapped.

Harry shook his head in amazement.

Behind him a door opened. Harry spun around to see a dapper, European-looking man with a small, neat trimmed mustache watching him.

"Who are you?" the man demanded.

"You Buchinski?"

The man's face became immediately wary. "You're trespassing, mister. This is private property."

"What are you, a lawyer?"

"Seeing as how you ask, yes, I am," Buchinski admitted. "Now whoever you are, you're disturbing these ladies and you're disturbing me."

"That's tough."

"I'm warning you, mister tough-guy. You better get your ass out of here while you can, or I'll have one of my associates rearrange your basic structure."

Harry stepped closer. "I'm looking for a tall brunette named Wanda. She used to work here."

"Yeah?"

"Tell me where I can find her and I'll leave. Otherwise I'm going to hang around for a while."

Buchinski's voice was confident. "Let me tell you something, punk. This place is a protected operation. If you think you can get tough around here, you go ahead and try. You'll end up with your balls in the spaghetti sauce."

"You mean you're going to put the hurt on me. Is that it?" Harry gave him a short nod. "I'll tell you something. I'm real scared."

"Jump back, little man," snapped Buchinski. "Don't come on big and bad with me. The shoes on my feet cost more than you make in a week."

"You're telling me you've got connections in the syndicate, and that gives you a lot of clout."

Buchinski sneered. "You bet your butt, friend. I've got enough clout to have you blown away with one phone call. So I suggest you move along right now, or you're liable to end up very wasted. *Capice*?"

Harry grabbed a handful of Buchinski's shirt front. "I'll tell you something, asshole. From where I stand, you're nothing but a cheap little maggot who sells dirty pictures."

At this moment the huge bouncer, Hughie, burst through the doorway. In his enormous hand was a baseball bat. He toyed with it as if it were a baton. "All right, boss," he growled. "I'll take care of this finocchio." He grinned nastily at Harry. "You shoulda stuck with the rubber dolly, sport. Now you're gonna get messed up real bad."

Harry let go of Buchinski's shirt and faced Hughie. Buchinski scuttled away into his office, slamming the door behind him. The little old ladies had all stopped writing and were watching the scene, petrified.

Hughie made his move. He charged straight at Harry, swinging the bat at his head. Harry sidestepped the broad move, driving a left into Hughie's big gut as he went past, then bringing a sharp judo chop down across the back of the bouncer's thick neck. Hughie continued forward under his own momentum, bounced off the wall, and dropped back onto the floor with a dull grunt. He twitched but did not rise.

"Big man," muttered Harry. He tried the door to Buchinski's office. It was locked. He braced himself, drew back one leg, then kicked just under the lock. The door smashed inwards, ripping loose from one hinge.

As Harry burst in, Buchinski backed away, suddenly dodging into the office bathroom. Harry leaped after him. Buchinski threw open the bathroom window and tried to climb out. Harry grabbed him by the scruff of the neck, dragged him back inside, and slammed him around the room from wall to wall. Buchinski collapsed in the corner. Harry dragged him to his feet.

"Going someplace, asshole?"

Buchinski's eyes looked as if they would pop out of his head. "Hughie! Hughie!"

"Hughie won't be coming. He's doing a little floor time." He banged Buchinski's head against the wall. "All right now. It's question-and-answer time. I want to know where Wanda is."

"Go to hell, punk!" screamed Buchinski. "I don't know any fucking Wanda."

"I'm not convinced," sighed Harry. He grabbed Buchinski by the hair, pulled him down to the floor, and shoved his face into the toilet bowl, holding it under the water. Buchinski struggled to get away, but Harry held him tightly. Finally Harry dragged him out and slammed him up against the wall again. Buchinski was coughing up water, gasping and choking.

"You just don't listen very good." Harry shook him back and forth. "But we'll try again. Where do I find Wanda?"

"Kiss my ass!"

Harry stuffed Buchinski's face down into the toilet again, holding him under a lot longer this time. When Harry pulled him out, Buchinski's face was turning blue.

"I don't like to keep repeating myself, but for your benefit I will. One more time. Wanda."

"I'm not going to tell you one goddamn thing! Not one goddamn thing!"

"If you don't talk, there won't be enough left of you when I'm through to flush down this toilet." Harry started to pull Buchinski's head down toward the porcelain bowl again.

"Wait . . . wait . . . I'll talk, man! I'll talk!"

Harry let go of Buchinski's hair. "Well, now, that's more like it. I'm listening."

"She . . . she quit a couple of weeks ago. She said she didn't like working here. Said she was going back to her boyfriend, this pimp named Bobby Maxwell. She said she had a better deal going—that she was going to get some money."

"Where do I find them?"

"I don't know an address—"

"What?" Harry started to pull Buchinski's face down again.

"Wait . . . I do know she's been hanging around this church down on Garvey. It's called St. Ambrose."

St. Ambrose! The name flashed through Harry's memory like a bolt of lightning. The church where he had finally cornered Henry Lee Caldwell. Christ, it had been there all the time. It hadn't been just an accident they ended up there. Caldwell was going there for help. The goddamn priest was in on it!

Harry let go of Buchinski's hair. "You really ought to get cleaned up," he advised calmly. "You're a mess."

"You bastard! You can't get away with this!"

"I just did."

Harry walked out of the bathroom and started for the office door. Hughie loomed suddenly in his path, holding his trusty baseball bat once more.

"Kiss the world good-bye, shithead!" Hughie hissed. He started for Harry, but slowly this time, having learned a lesson from their previous encounter.

Harry backed away into the bathroom. Buchinski was still propped up against the wall. Harry grabbed him by the arm and shoved him out the door, into Hughie. The bouncer pushed his boss aside like so much toilet paper, zeroing in on Harry again.

Looking around, Harry saw a toilet plunger by the sink. As Hughie charged, Harry snapped up the plunger and came out low and fast. Using the plunger as a baton, he caught the swinging bat as it arced down at his head. In a series of fast moves, he drove the plunger into Hughie's solar plexus, then cracked him in the face, smearing the bouncer's nose like jelly. Blood spurted from Hughie's nostrils, and once again he pitched over onto the hard floor.

Harry breathed a tired sigh. "Some guys just don't give up easy," he commented. He dropped the suction cup of the plunger onto Hughie's upturned face.

The door was full of old ladies who had watched Harry's performance with glittering eyes.

"That was beautiful!" said one.

Harry looked modest. "Nothing to it," he told her.

Fifteen

Sitting in a small, dark bar on Garvey Street, across from St. Ambrose, Harry nursed a glass of beer that had gone warm and flat and watched the television on the wall. It was spewing the same old story, the mayor's kidnapping. You couldn't get away from it. Wherever you went, people were talking about it. It poured endlessly from the radio and television and covered the front pages of the newspapers.

Harry thought of the media in basically unflattering terms. They were ghouls who fed garbage to the masses and ate the results in the form of profits. But you couldn't really blame them, he admitted to himself, because it was the people's tastes they catered to. Misery sold better than humor, tragedy was more popular than romance, war was more exciting than peace, and death was more thrilling than life. The media gave their audience exactly what they wanted.

"It has now been over forty-eight hours," the newscaster was saying, "since the city of San Francisco was shocked and outraged by the incredible broad-daylight kidnapping of our mayor. This morning reporter Linda Wong talked with Captain Bradford McKay of the police department about the report that another tape-recorded message has been received from the kidnappers . . ."

The familiar face of McKay abruptly filled the screen, looking haggard and more human than Harry had ever seen him look before. The bastard is learning what is means to work for a living, Harry thought.

The scene behind McKay was the hallway outside his office in the Hall of Justice. McKay was forcing his way through a mob of clamoring newspeople, Bressler following in his wake. A microphone was suddenly thrust into McKay's face from off screen. He glared at it as if it were offensive to him. He had obviously lost much of his taste for publicity in the last two days.

"Captain McKay! Captain McKay, please!" The microphone was being held by a pretty young Chinese newswoman. She thrust her way in front of McKay, momentarily blocking his progress. "Isn't it true that the police department has received another tape from the so-called People's Revolutionary Strike Force?"

McKay nodded briefly, a stiff-necked movement. "Yes, we have. We received it in the mail this morning." McKay nudged past and continued down the hall. The camera jiggled as the newswoman and cameraman struggled to follow.

"Do the police have any idea whether or not the mayor is still all right?"

"We believe he is."

"Why is that?"

"Because they have assured us he is in good health," McKay said shortly.

"And you trust their word?"

"At this point we have little choice but to take their word for it."

"Then it is possible the mayor might be dead?"

"No comment."

"Is the city going to pay the ransom demand?"

"Yes, we are." McKay took a breath. "There won't be any payment or arrangement for transportation out of the country until we've actually seen the mayor with our own eyes and are absolutely sure he is alive and well."

"Then you have decided to let the kidnappers go?"

"It's one of their demands. Under the circumstances, we have very little choice in the matter. The mayor will not actually be set free until the kidnappers are on board the plane with the money."

Another reporter shoved his way up to McKay, pushing his microphone in. "Captain McKay, there is a rumor circulating that the police actually know where the kidnappers are hiding but are doing nothing about it for fear of endangering the mayor's life. Is that true?"

"No, absolutely false! That rumor is a bunch of— is totally wrong. We are, however, expecting one more message this afternoon telling us the time and place for delivery."

"Captain McKay—"

"I'm afraid that's all I have time for right now. If you'll excuse me . . ."

McKay and Bressler broke through the crowd and stepped into a waiting elevator being held open by a young policeman. As the doors slid closed, the picture cut back to the television station newsroom and the newscaster again. "In other news this evening there was renewed violence in the Mideast . . ."

Harry drained his glass.

"You ask me, they can keep the dumb son of a bitch!" It was the bartender talking. He leaned across the bar and fixed his eyes on Harry, speaking with a confidence gained through years spent giving advice to drunks. "Hell, I didn't even vote for the jerk. Myself, I always go straight Democrat. Ever since he got into office, which had to be a mistake at the polls, this goddamn city has been going downhill. Me and my wife, we own a house just around the corner. Our property assessment has practically doubled in the last three years, and I want you to know it has nothing to do with improvements. I ain't made any improvements on that house in I don't know how long, so why does the assessment keep getting bigger all the time? I'll tell you why. It's the mayor. He's in charge. So if it isn't his fault, whose fault is it? And now he's going to cost two million dollars to get back. The only way he'd be worth that much is if we gave it to those guys that snatched him and said go ahead, drop the bastard in the Bay. Now that might be worth the money." He paused, waiting for Harry to say something. Harry had nothing to say. The bartender took the empty glass. "You want another one?"

"Sure."

The bartender walked away with Harry's glass.

The door opened, letting in the harsh glare of sunlight. Kate came in, looked around, spotted Harry, and walked over to take a stool beside him. The bartender raised his eyebrows at Harry and stuck up two fingers quizzically. Harry nodded. The bartender drew a second beer, thunked them down, and took his money.

Kate waited until they were alone at the end of the bar.

"Hello, Harry."

Harry nodded without speaking.

"Sorry I'm late. It took a little longer to get through those records than I thought it would. You know how many peple there are in San Francisco named Voss?" She took a thick manila envelope from her purse, bent back the brass fasteners, and tugged out a thick sheaf of papers.

"What did you find?" Harry asked.

"I think you'll be interested. That priest at St. Ambrose, Father John Voss? Well, he's very militant, very big in prison reform. He headed one of those private organizations which filed a report with the governor very critical of California's penal institutions. He holds seminars in rehabilitation at all the prisons around the area. Soledad, Santa Rita, San Quentin. He's not very popular with the wardens, but he seems to be able to put the right kind of pressure in the right places to hold his programs." She thumbed through her papers until she found the particular one she was looking for. Harry drained half his beer while she searched. Kate held out the sheet. "This is the one you're really going to like. It's a list of prisoners who took Voss's seminars. One of them was Bobby Maxwell."

Harry glanced down the list until he found the name. "He was in prison?" he asked with some surprise.

Kate nodded. "Uh-huh. From nineteen seventy-two to nineteen seventy-four. For armed robbery of a gas station down on Geary. It was his first offense, so he received a light sentence. Looks like he's graduated to bigger things. Kidnapping the mayor is quite a step up. I guess he got greedy."

Harry finished his beer. "Well, I guess that wraps it," he decided. "The priest has been covering for them. It was there all the time, right under my nose, and I missed it."

"Everybody missed it," Kate pointed out quietly. "You aren't the only one."

"I think I'll go over and have a little heart-to-heart with our friend Father John."

Kate put the papers back in the envelope. "Want me to come along?"

Harry stood up. "No, you stay here. This is going to be a very private conversation. You sit tight and drink your beer."

"I don't like beer."

"Have a Coke, then."

"You never change, do you?" asked Kate. "You still think I'll get in the way."

"No, I just think you could get in a lot of hot water if you get in any trouble with a suspended officer breaking a few rules. Especially if the officer happens to be me."

"You think I care about that, Harry?"

"I care about it."

Harry found Father John Voss kneeling before the altar of the church, praying quietly.

"Hello there, Father John."

The priest looked up, startled.

"Praying for forgiveness?"

Seeing Harry, the priest's eyes grew angry. "You! What do you want?"

"Remember me, father?"

"Yes, I remember you only too well, I'm afraid.

You're the policeman who arrested that poor man. And brutally beat him without any reason."

"Not exactly without reason. He put a bomb in the Hall of Justice that could have killed a lot of innocent people. You were in on it with him, father. Two days ago his friends kidnapped the mayor and murdered seven people. You were in on that, too. You've been in on it all from the beginning."

Father John jumped to his feet, glaring at Harry. "What right do you have to harass me in my own church? Or don't you recognize any authority higher than your gun?"

"You're a fine one to talk about guns, aren't you? Considering how many people your friends have killed." Harry's voice was quiet but full of menace. "I'm through playing games with you. It's time you and I had a little talk. I want to know about the mayor, and I want to know about Bobby Maxwell."

The priest pushed past him. "I don't have to answer your questions—or your insinuations. Get a warrant!"

As Father John started down the aisle a nun came in from a side door and sat in the pews. She bowed her head in an attitude of prayer.

Harry ran after the priest, grabbing his arm, spinning him around. "Just a minute, father. I'm not through talking to you yet."

"I thought I made myself clear to you, officer. I have nothing to say to you whatsoever. And I resent your intrusion into my church. You are not welcome here. Now I think you had better leave before I call your superiors and file a formal complaint."

"You want to make a complaint, you go right ahead. Maxwell and the rest of those bastards killed a good friend of mine. I'm not going to let them get away with it."

"I've had enough of your threats. I'm asking you to leave for the last time."

Harry nodded at a booth against the wall. "That's a confessional, isn't it?"

"Yes. Why? Do you want to make a confession?"

"Why don't you go first? Where's Bobby Maxwell?"

172

"Do you really think I'll tell you that?"

Harry stiffened with anger. "Why not? What are you protecting him for? What makes Maxwell worth it, a murdering bastard like that? You call yourself a man of God! What about that part in the Bible that says, 'Thou shalt not kill'? That doesn't count for anything? Do you know how many people Maxwell's group has killed? And they'll kill more! For what? So they can split the country and live high on the hog with their two million dollars! How does that all figure, father?"

"Sacrifices have to be made sometimes . . ."

"Sacrifices?" Harry was outraged.

"In the cause of peace."

"Kids burned up in a station wagon? What kind of cause does that serve? If you have to do things like that to win, then you become worse than the people you're supposed to be fighting."

Father John's face became hard. "I don't expect you to understand. These people are at war."

"So am I!" snarled Harry. "And you just might be the first casualty!"

"I'm not afraid of you—"

"No?" Harry suddenly shoved the priest backwards into the confessional booth. He tugged out his big Magnum and jammed it into Father John's face. "All right, father, if you don't talk now, so help me God—"

"How dare you!" gasped the priest. "How dare you pull a gun in the House of God! Have you no respect for or belief in the sanctity of the Church?"

"What about the sanctity of life? Or don't you believe in that any more?"

At the back of the church Harry saw the nun in the pews stand up. She was watching them. She started down the aisle toward the confessional.

"I believe that God in his Wisdom understands what I must do."

Harry shook the priest hard, cutting him off. "I haven't got time to debate religion with you now. Now where is Bobby Maxwell? Tell me, damn you, or I swear before God that I'll use this gun on you!"

173

"You wouldn't dare!"

"It's a hard way to find out, father."

"I won't—I can't—"

The nun seemed to be reaching into the folds of her habit, pulling something out. The movement distracted Harry. As he turned to see what she was doing, there was the sound of a shot. It echoed through the silence of the church like an explosion. The nun staggered forward, clutching at one of the benches for support. Then she fell forward onto the floor. Behind her, framed in the open doorway, stood Kate, legs in a wide stance, her smoking service revolver held stiffly in both hands.

"My God!" cried Father John, horrified. He pushed out of the confessional, past Harry, and ran to the fallen nun. Harry followed him.

"What have you done?" the priest demanded as Kate walked up. "You've killed her!"

Kate lowered the revolver slowly. Her hands were shaking, and her face had gone pale and bloodless. "How . . . how many nuns do you know with red fingernails?" she asked in a quivering voice.

Harry bent forward and rolled the nun over onto her back. He tugged the twisted habit aside. The girl wearing it was young, a tall brunette. Her fingernails were long and red. Under the habit she was wearing a pullover shirt and blue jeans. There was something else hidden under the folds of her costume. Harry picked it up. It was a twelve-gauge pump shotgun.

"She was going to kill you," said Kate. "I never shot anybody before, Harry."

"She was going to kill both of us," said Harry. "You, too, father. Why do you think she was here? You know too much now. They can't trust you any more."

Father John looked at Harry with vacant eyes. He fell to his knees beside the girl's body. "Wanda," he whispered, taking her lifeless hand, clutching it between his own. His eyes filled with tears. "There was never supposed to be any killing," he whispered. "They promised me no one would get hurt."

"You knew what was going on," said Harry. "You knew."

"Yes, I knew." Father John closed his eyes and crossed himself. "Holy Father in Heaven, forgive me."

Harry grabbed the priest and dragged him to his feet. "You can't close your eyes this time, father. Now where are they holding the mayor?"

For a moment Father John seemed unable to speak. When he spoke his voice was dry and lifeless.

"Alcatraz . . . they're on Alcatraz . . ."

Sixteen

In 1775, Spanish explorers entering San Francisco Bay for the first time discovered a small island covered with pelicans. They decided to name it *Isla de los Alcatraces*, which means Island of the Pelicans. In 1848, the island was sold to the U.S. government for five thousand dollars and shortly thereafter a military fort was constructed by army engineers. The island remained under army jurisdiction until 1934, when the War Department decided Alcatraz was no longer necessary for defense and transferred it to the Department of Justice. Its isolated, impregnable situation in the middle of the bay made it an ideal location for a maximum security prison, which it remained for thirty years—an infamous, fortress-like penitentiary known as "The Rock," where only the most dangerous and hardened criminals were sent. There is no record of a successful escape from Alcatraz, though numerous attempts were made. One inmate actually made it to Fort Point, at the base of the Golden Gate Bridge. Naked, exhausted from the swim, he was recaptured. To date, five escaped prisoners are still unaccounted for, but it is believed that they died trying to swim the treacherous currents surrounding the island.

In 1963, Alcatraz was finally closed as a prison, an act many humanitarian penologists strongly favored. It remained unoccupied until 1969, when a band of militant Indians took possession of the island, claiming that it had been given to their people as part of yet another government treaty which was never honored. Hopes of creating an Indian cultural center there were dashed in 1971, when the Indians were at last forced by U.S. marshals to abandon the island. Since that time it has remained uninhabited, a grim symbol of a bygone part of America's history.

From the upper deck of the police fireboat *Barbary Coast*, Harry and Kate watched Alcatraz come closer and closer.

"You sure you don't want me to call in for a backup on this, Inspector Callahan?" asked the fireboat skipper, a big, burly man built like a stevedore.

"Just get me on the island," Harry told him. "There's no time for a backup to be any help, anyway."

"Okay. It's your show." The skipper stepped back into the bridge cabin.

"He's right," said Kate when the skipper was out of hearing range. "We should call in and let the department handle this."

"And do what?" Harry demanded. "They're prepared to give those bastards two million dollars and let them go. I'm not about to let that happen."

"We could screw it up. We could get the mayor killed."

"They won't kill him. He's their ace in the hole, their ticket to freedom. Once he's dead, they can kiss their escape and the money good-bye. No, they won't kill him. They're not dumb. They'll fight like hell to keep him, though."

Kate had another thought. "We could get killed."

"Not *we*," said Harry dourly. "Me. I go alone on this one."

"But—"

"No buts. This is personal." Harry's look at her was almost kindly. "Face it, you don't have the experience. You said yourself you never killed anybody before."

"If I hadn't been in that church," she countered, "you might be dead right now."

"I appreciate what you did. Look, I'm not knocking

it. You handled it good. But these guys are tough professionals. They were in Vietnam together. They know what guerrilla warfare is all about. If I have to keep looking out for you, it's only going to slow me down. And it could get both of us killed. You want that? I'm going to have enough to worry about with the mayor. They'll try to use him as a shield, and I've got to prevent that. When that helicopter appears at four o'clock, all hell is going to break loose."

"All the more reason to bring me. Two guns are better than one, right?"

Harry shook his head adamantly. "Wrong. You're not going, and that's it."

Kate brushed her blowing hair out of her face. "All right then, how about this? You're on suspension. When McKay finds out about this, about how you disobeyed his orders, he'll crucify you. Now, I'm still on duty—"

"All the more reason for you not to come. If I screw this up, and I'm not dead, McKay will nail my nuts to the nearest door. I don't want you caught up in that."

Kate grinned. "I'm not worried. I'm a woman. I haven't got nuts."

Harry didn't laugh. "He could still nail what you've got. The answer is no."

"Sometimes, Inspector Callahan, you can be awfully difficult."

A flicker of a smile crossed Harry's face. "You haven't seen anything yet, baby."

"We just received the last tape," the chief told McKay and Bressler. They were standing in the chief's inner office. The clock on the wall said three-thirty.

"What's the deal?" asked McKay.

"They're holding him on Alcatraz. We're to deliver the money in half an hour."

McKay's face was knife sharp. "I'd like the job, sir."

"I thought you would," said the chief. "It's yours."

McKay suppressed a smile. He could see his name in the headlines now. It was exactly the kind of boost his career could use. And it would look good in his file when the day came that the chief finally retired and they were choosing a successor.

"I've got the helicopter upstairs on standby. The money is right here." The chief nodded at two black satchels on his desk. "You'll fly over the island. The helicopter will drop you in the prison exercise yard on the north end of the island and take off again. You'll meet the kidnappers, have them take you to the mayor, and see that he's all right. If he is, you'll signal, and the helicopter will land again. It will ferry all of you to the Oakland airport. We picked Oakland because it's less crowded. A 707 is waiting there to take them anywhere they want to go."

A shadow passed behind the chief's eyes. He looked troubled.

"Something wrong, sir?" McKay asked.

It was a moment before the answer came. "I just hope to God we're doing the right thing."

"We don't have any choice, sir, under the circumstances."

The chief's eyes moved past him to the window. From where he was standing he could just make out the pyramid-shaped TransAmerica Building. Beyond that, he knew, in almost a straight line, was Alcatraz.

When he spoke again, his voice was as distant as an echo. "I wonder . . ."

From his cell window the mayor could see a patch of blue sky and nothing else. At night he could hear the crash of waves breaking on the rocks. It was the waves that told him where he was. On Alcatraz, that had to be it. Shortly after he had been forced to board the motorboat three days ago, he had been tied, gagged, and blindfolded by the one with the Southern accent, the one they called Tex. The blindfold had not been removed until the mayor was in his cell. But it was easy enough to figure out. They had only been on the boat a short while, not more than fifteen minutes, and it had taken just a few minutes for them to lead him to his cell. It had to be Alcatraz. Deserted, isolated, a fortress. A perfect spot for them to hide until the money was paid and he was finally released.

And he would be released, of that he was certain. The money would be paid, his family would take care of that. The kidnappers had no reason to kill him. They would have to trade him for their freedom. Even once the money was paid, they would need him alive to guarantee their own safety. Once they were on board the plane they would let him go, he had been told that. And he believed it. It was really just a matter of waiting . . .

Even believing this, the mayor had an uneasy feeling in his stomach. The leader, the one they called Bobby, frightened him. He was mad, there was no doubt about that. There was a strange look in the man's eyes, a far-away look of unmistakable insanity. When Bobby looked at him, it was a ravenous wolf looking at a lamb ready for slaughter. He knew Bobby would not hesitate to kill him if the necessity came, would in fact enjoy it.

Clasping his hands together in sudden terror, the mayor began to pray . . .

The fireboat slowly circled Alcatraz, one hundred yards off the island. As it swung around the southern tip, the dock came into view.

"Drop me there," Harry instructed the skipper.

The skipper passed the order on to the helmsman. The bow of the big fireboat came about and nosed in toward the dock.

From his vantage point in the lighthouse, near the main cell block, Tex could see the entire island laid out before him. He watched the fireboat on its slow run past the island without much interest. In his three days as lookout, he had gotten used to boats coming in close to the island. Nothing to worry about. It was nearly four o'clock, anyhow. In a few minutes the helicopter would deliver the money, and they would be on their way. Everything had worked perfectly so far, exactly as Bobby had planned it. Tex was certain the rest would go like a piece of cake. The helicopter would take them to the airport and a waiting jetliner. Bobby would give the pilot exact flying instructions. Somewhere over Montana the plane would cut its speed and drop down to one thousand feet. They would parachute out and disappear into the woods where nobody would ever find them. Bobby had a friend in southern Montana who was a private pilot and owned his own plane. They would find the man, who, for twenty thousand dollars, would fly them to Canada. From there they would go to Europe and lie low for three or four months. After that, anywhere they wanted.

Tex reached into his shirt pocket, taking a cigarette out of the pack nestled there. He struck a match and took a deep drag. All he could think about was the money. Two million split five ways came to four hundred thousand dollars each. With that kind of bread he would buy himself a plantation in South America and spend the rest of his life as a fat, rich *gringo*.

Something caught his attention. What the hell?

It was the fireboat. It was turning in to the island, pulling up to the dock. Holy Christ!

As the boat eased up against the old cement pier, Harry galloped down the companionway to the main deck, clambered over the port railing, and jumped ashore. He looked back and saw Kate watching him from the upper deck, her face full of concern.

"Take care of yourself!" she called.

Harry flashed her a confident smile that he did not feel, then turned to face the island. Ahead of him was a big, four-story, rectangular building. Having checked one of the fireboat's maps of Alcatraz, Harry knew the building to be the guard's barracks. Beyond that, a hill rose to the center of the island. Just past the barracks, up a slight incline, was a fortified arch which could be closed off with a big steel gate—in the old days this had been used to keep prisoners from trying to escape when the supply ship was docked. Beyond this was the burned-out recreation center. A switchback road led up the hill. At the top Harry could see the lighthouse and the grim main cellblock building. That, he thought, was where they would be holding the mayor.

With a last glance at the fireboat, Harry started up the road.

Tex saw a big man in a leather jacket jump off the fireboat onto the dock. The man hesitated, then started toward the old barracks building and the road. Then Tex saw the man reach into his jacket and pull out a gun, a big revolver with a long barrel. Christ, a cop! A goddamn cop!

Tex picked up the AR-15 on the stone floor at his feet. He watched the big man disappear behind the barracks building. He waited a fraction of a second more, then dropped the cigarette, crushing it out with the heel of his cowboy boot. He twisted the automatic rifle sling around his forearm to steady his aim, in the military manner.

He waited.

At the railing of the fireboat, Kate watched until Harry disappeared up the road.

"Prepare to cast off!" shouted the skipper.

"Wait a minute!" cried Kate. "I'm getting off, too!" She hurried down the companionway and jumped onto the dock.

The engines of the fireboat roared. The big vessel slowly eased away from the cement pier. Churning water, the fireboat nosed out into the bay.

Kate pulled out her service revolver, snapped open the cylinder, popped out the one expended shell, and slipped in a fresh cartridge.

She squinted up the hill. From here on, it was just the two of them, her and Harry. Against an army.

At the top of the hill, the first buildings Harry saw were the burned-out remains of the warden's residence and the rebuilt lighthouse. Both had accidentally been burned down by the Indians in 1970, when a fire had gotten out of control. The lighthouse now operated mechanically.

Harry stopped, staring up at the lighthouse tower. If Bobby Maxwell was smart, he would have a lookout up there. Which meant they probably knew he was here.

Seconds later, there was no doubt. The staccato sound of an automatic rifle came sharply, and a line of bullets chewed across the pavement in front of him. Harry dived out of the way as the bullets cut past him. He rolled behind the corner of the warden's house and came up in a crouch.

Silently, Harry made his way around to the back of the warden's home. Over the years weeds had sprouted up everywhere, overgrowing the concrete around the residence and the lighthouse. Harry reached the opposite corner of the house in time to see a tall man with an AR-15 moving around the top walkway of the lighthouse.

Harry sighted the big Magnum at the searchlight housing. In a few moments the tall man reappeared, eyes searching the courtyard for Harry.

Harry squeezed the trigger. BOOM!

Tex stood there for what seemed like an eternity, swaying in the wind. His body pitched forward over the railing and fell. With a sickening thud, he hit the pavement a dozen feet from where Harry stood, arms and legs splayed out at impossible angles.

Harry did not bother to check the body, knowing that such a fall could only result in death. He ran for the main cell block building entrance.

In the administration office, Bobby, Lalo, and Karl heard the shooting.

"Christ!" swore Bobby. "It's Tex—somebody's on the island!"

"It must be the goddamn cops," Lalo said.

Bobby jerked his thumb at the door. "Karl, get out there and find out what's going on. Lalo, go get the mayor." Bobby crossed to a big transceiver on one of the tables. "I'll try to get the helicopter on the radio and find out what the hell is going on."

Karl picked up an AR-15, checked the clip, and went out.

Harry searched a maze of corridors and hallways in the main building, finding nothing. Ahead he saw a stairway. As he reached it, he heard running footsteps from the basement. He hesitated, then went down.

From the bottom of the stairs he followed a long hallway to a shadowy shower room. He froze in the doorway, his eyes searching the room. Whoever was down here could be hiding in any one of a dozen dark places. Cautiously, Harry moved along the wall.

A whisper of sound caught his attention. Harry turned, and saw Karl in the doorway behind him. The AR-15 in Karl's hands chattered noisily. Bullets ripped past Harry's head, blasting pieces out of the wall behind him.

Harry dropped to his hands and knees. He skidded across the cement floor, Magnum clutched in both hands. Unprepared for this sudden move, Karl tried to swing the AR-15 around to cover him. Harry rolled to the side, firing the forty-four twice. The bullets slammed into Karl's chest, knocking him backward through the doorway. The barrel of his automatic rifle went up, firing. It went on firing until the clip had been expended.

Harry scrambled to his feet. He found Karl lying on his back in the hallway, staring sightlessly at the ceiling he had just blasted. There seemed to be a slight smile on his lips, almost as if he understood this to be some absurd joke.

Harry started back down the hallway. Somewhere in the building he heard the unmistakable sound of gunfire.

He ran for the stairs.

Lalo unlocked the door of the mayor's cell and dragged it open. He unslung his rifle and jabbed the barrel at the mayor's chest.

"Let's go!"

Terrified, the mayor cowered in the corner. "Where?"

"On a fucking picnic!" Lalo snarled. He grabbed the mayor by the jacket and dragged him out of the cell. Not bothering to close the door, Lalo gave the mayor a shove. "Move it!"

They started along the corridor which led to the prison's administration offices. Suddenly, behind them, they heard a woman shout.

"Police! Put up your hands!"

The mayor and Lalo turned to see Kate Moore at the far end of the corridor, her service revolver trained on them.

Lalo studied Kate with cold eyes, but did not move.

"Drop the weapon!" snapped Kate. "I won't tell you again!"

Slowly, Lalo started to lower the barrel of the automatic rifle. Then, suddenly, he brought the AR-15 up. Kate fired from the hip. The bullet hit Lalo in the stomach, punching him backward. He collapsed, his weapon skidding across the cement floor. He did not move again.

"Inspector Moore!" whispered the mayor, in his tone a mixture of gratitude and hysteria. "Thank God you've come! I was afraid they were going to kill me—"

Kate grabbed him by the arm and dragged him toward the corridor. "Come with me, Your Honor—I'll get us both out of here."

They hurried down the corridor. Bobby Maxwell appeared in a doorway. Kate saw him and tried to bring up her revolver, but could not move fast enough. Bobby's automatic rifle blasted across her body. Kate fell to her knees, covered with blood. She looked up at the mayor with a quizzical expression, and then fell forward onto her face.

The mayor began to scream. To quiet him, Bobby smashed the butt of the AR-15 across his face. The mayor staggered back from the blow and fell against the bars of a cell.

"Don't give me any of your shit!" Bobby snarled viciously. "Or I'll blow your fucking head off right now!"

He grabbed the mayor by the hair and jammed the barrel of the rifle against the side of his head.

"D-don't kill me!" moaned the mayor in stark terror.

"Come on!" growled Bobby, dragging the mayor toward the door. "Your goddamn friends better show up with that money in five minutes, or I'm going to splatter your brains all over this island!"

Harry found Kate's body sprawled in the main cell block. He crouched beside her, cradling her in his arms. Her eyes were glazed, unable to focus. She was dying.

"Harry?" she whispered.

Harry forced a crooked grin. "Who else?"

Kate tried to smile but couldn't. "I didn't do bad . . . did I?"

Harry gritted his teeth. "No," he heard himself saying. "Not bad at all. You did just fine."

But Kate could not hear him. She was dead.

Slowly, carefully, tenderly, Harry lowered her to the floor. He looked over at Lalo's body.

One more. Bobby Maxwell.

Bobby dragged the mayor down a narrow corridor containing solitary confinement cells, then through an open doorway which led outside. A dozen stone steps opened out into the prisoner's exercise ground, a long, empty yard surrounded by high concrete walls.

Bobby's eyes searched the yard and found what they were looking for—a guard tower in the corner.

"Come on, you fat bastard!" he told the mayor. "I want you up where they can see you!"

He dragged the mayor to the base of the guard tower. A stairway led up to a platform which had once served as a lookout point for the guards to watch exercising prisoners.

"Up!" growled Bobby, shoving the mayor. They went up a few steps, and then the mayor hung his head over the railing and vomited from fear.

"You stinking fat bastard! Up those stairs, or I swear to God I'll shoot you right now!"

The mayor retched again. "I can't," he muttered hysterically. "Please . . . I can't '. . ."

And then they heard it, the sound of the helicopter, distant at first, but the chatter of its blades growing steadily in volume.

"It's coming," said Bobby in a hushed voice. "You hear that? It's coming!"

Momentarily forgetting the mayor, he clambered up the rest of the stairs to the top of the tower. On the platform, he stood waving his hands at the approaching helicopter.

Maxwell!"

Bobby looked down to see a big man on the stone steps below, staring up at him.

"They're all dead!" the big man shouted. "It's just you and me now . . . punk!"

Bobby squinted at the big man. He was holding something in his hands—a long, dark green tube.

For the first time in his life, Bobby felt fear in the pit of his stomach. It was a LAWS rocket.

Bobby screamed. *"No—God—no!"*

Harry jerked up the weapon 'and fired. The flaming rocket streaked toward the top of the tower. When it hit, the entire top of the tower exploded in a ball of fire. Pieces of Bobby's burning body rained through the air like dozens of fiery comets.

Harry dropped the rocket launcher. The mayor staggered across the yard to greet him.

"Callahan! Callahan! You saved my life! I'll see that you get another commendation for this!"

The mayor stopped in mid-step, halted by Harry's expression of cold hatred. He decided he'd better not say any more.

The chatter of the helicopter became deafening. Harry saw it appear overhead, hovering like a giant metal bird. A figure leaned out of the cockpit, holding a bullhorn.

"Helicopter to revolutionary group!"

Harry recognized McKay's voice.

"Helicopter to revolutionary group! We are ready to touch down! We have the money!"

Harry turned away and walked back into the building. He found Kate where he had left her. Her eyes were closed, her face almost peaceful in death.

He knelt beside her, cradling her body in his arms. His eyes filled with tears.

THRILLERS

Δ	0352397012	George Arnaud **WAGES OF FEAR**	70p*
Δ	0352303077	**DICK BARTON SPECIAL AGENT** Mike Dorrell **No. 1: THE GREAT TOBACCO CONSPIRACY**	60p
Δ	0352303085	**No. 2: THE MYSTERY OF THE MISSING FORMULA**	60p
Δ	0352303093	Alan Radnor **No. 3: THE CASE OF THE VANISHING HOUSE**	60p
Δ	0352303107	Larry Pryce **No. 4: THE GOLD BULLION SWINDLE**	70p
Δ	0352303468	Murray Teigh Bloom **LAST EMBRACE**	90p*
	0352396474	Paul Bonnecarrere **ULTIMATUM**	95p
	0352302607	**THE GOLDEN TRIANGLE**	95p
	0352304502	**THE LOST VICTORY**	95p
	0352396059	Richard Butler **WHERE ALL THE GIRLS ARE SWEETER**	95p
	0352395354	**ITALIAN ASSETS**	95p
	0352396067	Henry Denker **THE PHYSICIANS**	95p*
	0352300523	**A PLACE FOR THE MIGHTY**	75p*
	0352302127	Robert Early **A TIME OF MADNESS**	75p
	0352304588	John Gardner **UNDERSTRIKE**	95p
	035230460X	**AMBER NINE**	95p
	0352304596	**MADRIGAL**	95p
	0352304618	**FOUNDER MEMBER**	95p
	0352398582	Burt Hirschfeld **'FATHER PIG'**	95p*
	0352395176	**SECRETS**	95p*
	0352398604	**BEHOLD ZION**	95p*
	0427004306	William Hughes **SPLIT ON RED**	95p
	0427004438	**COVER ZERO**	95p

GENERAL FICTION

Δ	042697114X	Cyril Abraham **THE ONEDIN LINE: THE SHIPMASTER**	**80p**
Δ	0426132661	**THE ONEDIN LINE: THE IRON SHIPS**	**80p**
Δ	042616184X	**THE ONEDIN LINE: THE HIGH SEAS**	**80p**
Δ	0426172671	**THE ONEDIN LINE: THE TRADE WINDS**	**80p**
Δ	0352304006	**THE ONEDIN LINE: THE WHITE SHIPS**	**95p**
	0352302550	Spiro T. Agnew **THE CANFIELD DECISION**	**£1.25***
	0352302690	Lynne Reid Banks **MY DARLING VILLAIN**	**85p**
	0352304251	T. G. Barclay **A SOWER WENT FORTH**	**£1.95**
Δ	0352302747	Michael J. Bird **THE APHRODITE INHERITANCE**	**85p**
	0352302712	Judy Blume **FOREVER**	**75p***
Δ	0352305355	John Brason **SECRET ARMY: THE END OF THE LINE**	**75p**
	0352303441	Barbara Brett **BETWEEN TWO ETERNITIES**	**75p***
	0352305916	André Brink **RUMOURS OF RAIN**	**£1.95**
	0352302003	Jeffrey Caine **HEATHCLIFF**	**75p**
	0352395168	**THE COLD ROOM**	**85p**
	0352304987	Ramsey Campbell **THE DOLL WHO ATE HIS MOTHER**	**95p***
	0352305398	**THE FACE THAT MUST DIE**	**95p**
	0352300647	**DEMONS BY DAYLIGHT**	**95p***

BARBARA CARTLAND'S ANCIENT WISDOM SERIES

	0427004209	Barbara Cartland **THE FORGOTTEN CITY**	**70p***
	0427004217	L. Adams Beck **THE HOUSE OF FULFILMENT**	**70p***
	0427004225	Marie Corelli **A ROMANCE OF TWO WORLDS**	**70p***
	0427004233	Talbot Mundy **BLACK LIGHT**	**70p***
	0427004241	L. Adams Beck **THE GARDEN OF VISION**	**70p***

† For sale in Britain and Ireland only.
* Not for sale in Canada. ● Reissues.
Δ Film & T.V. tie-ins.

Wyndham Books are obtainable from many booksellers and newsagents. If you have any difficulty please send purchase price plus postage on the scale below to:

Wyndham Cash Sales
P.O. Box 11
Falmouth
Cornwall
OR
Star Book Service,
G.P.O. Box 29,
Douglas,
Isle of Man,
British Isles.

While every effort is made to keep prices low, it is sometimes necessary to increase prices at short notice. Wyndham Books reserve the right to show new retail prices on covers which may differ from those advertised in the text or elsewhere.

Postage and Packing Rate

UK: 22p for the first book, plus 10p per copy for each additional book ordered to a maximum charge of 82p. **BFPO and Eire:** 22p for the first book, plus 10p per copy for the next 6 books and thereafter 4p per book. **Overseas:** 30p for the first book and 10p per copy for each additional book.

These charges are subject to Post Office charge fluctuations.